I0689732

SILENT NIGHT

BY
NICOLE R. KOBROWSKI

UNSEENPRESS.COM, INC.
WESTFIELD, INDIANA

This book is a work of fiction. Unless otherwise indicated, all the names,
characters, businesses, places, events, and incidents in this book are
either the product of the author's imagination or used in a fictitious
manner. Any resemblance to actual persons, living or dead, or actual
events is purely coincidental. The opinions expressed are those of the
characters and should not be confused with the author's opinions.
Although this book mentions real places, none of the events, real or
imagined, happened at these places.

Library of Congress Cataloging-in-Publication Data

Kobrowski, Nicole
  Silent Night
  1. Ghosts Indiana; 2. Paranormal Indiana ;3. Fiction; 4.Suspense

Library of Congress Control Number: 2021907355
ISBN 978-1-951437-00-8

Printed in the United States of America

Published by
Unseenpress.com, Inc.
PO Box 687
Westfield, IN 46074

Although the authors and publisher have made every effort to ensure the
accuracy and completeness of information contained in this book, we assume
no responsibility for errors, inaccuracies, omissions or any inconsistency
herein. Any slights of people, places or organizations are unintentional.

Cover design by Unseenpress.com, Inc.

DEDICATION

To everything
that happened
for a reason,
without which
this book
would not be.

Everything is as it should be.

Table of Contents

ONE

Now and then, a noise that sounded like a cat being tortured ensued from somewhere within the house. The person listened carefully. Yes! There it was again.

Stealthily, the tall form walked silently through the house as if it belonged there. The dark-clad figure stopped by the television and looked at the pictures there. So many pretty girls lived here— seven in all. The intruder knew that they shared the house in conjunction with some sort of religious counseling. The house was a much more private space than living on campus, and the encroacher knew that the girls didn't have to pay rent. At least not in cold, hard cash.

The house itself was structurally sound. The midnight visitor knew that from the many times it had been in the place, but the interior was full of poorly repaired walls and questionable plumbing. But it worked for the soon-to-graduate women who jokingly talked about "roughing it". Indeed they paid the price for living off-campus.

Sneaking quietly into the kitchen, it

passed by the ancient but functional washing machine. Piles of clean clothes were arranged neatly in seven pigeonholes that were assigned a name for each girl. Two tubs of dirty laundry sat next to the scarred almond-colored machine.

Panties.

Yum.

It wouldn't do to be discovered, but the lithe shape could not resist lifting a silky peach pair from the top of the pile and breathing in their perfume. The figure smiled as it thought about what had been in those panties not too long ago.

And again.

Letting the cold panties fall reluctantly from frozen hands, the dark outlined figure picked up what was needed and wrapped it.

Again.

It turned towards the noise which was like the sweetest, titillating symphony carried over the quiet house on the wings of darkness. It moved back into the living room and looked down the hall. Except for the flickering light underneath an old wooden door, the house could have been abandoned for the evening. Its smile split the darkness as it licked full sensuous lips.

Showtime.

Creeping closer to the hallway, the trespasser could see that the door was closed. Another low wail let the figure know that this was the right direction. It continued closer to the noise. Excitement coursed hotly through a body temporarily incapable of warmth.

Kneeling, the shadow looked in an old-fashioned skeleton keyhole.

No key? Tsk tsk. You really should be more careful. The figure put its eye directly on the hole and peered in. What it saw made the figure grip the handle of the silk-covered knife.

On the low bed were two figures passionately entwined. The woman had her tanned legs on both sides of the man's slim hips moving between her legs. His head was buried in her neck, and the figure could hear him whispering to her.

The figure saw the dark-haired woman wrap her legs around the man and stifle another cry in his shoulder.

Suddenly, the figure at the door dropped the package, and it landed with a thud on the old wooden floor. In a split second, the figure saw the man and woman turn towards the door with a mix of surprise and concern. Rage twisted deeply inside the midnight interloper.

"What's going on here?" a sleepy voice called from behind a door.

Soon lights could be seen glowing, and doors were opening all along the long corridor.

The girl who had spoken, Tiffanie, yawned, "Can't we get some sleep here? I've got a biology test tomorrow, and it counts for half of my grade! We get enough interrupted sleep as it is!"

"Really!" another complained. "Someone here needs to tone it down. I don't care who you have in your room, but for God's sake, keep the noise down!"

Lena, a liberal arts major, stepped out of her room and stopped short. "Hey, what the hell is this?" She was out of breath with a sheet wrapped around her.

The other girls came out of their rooms and gathered around Lena.

"Whose scarf is this?" someone demanded. "What the hell is a knife doing here?"

"It's Joy's favorite!" Joy, another liberal arts major, was known for her colorful and flamboyant dress and her love of pranks.

"Joy! That isn't cool, not at all!"

"Yeah, that's way uncool."

"Worse than that, it's sick!"

"Sicker than normal, you mean!"

"Joy, this kind of prank isn't funny!" Lena held the scarf out to a dumbstruck Joy.

Joy took the scarf from Lena and looked at the knife. "I didn't do it, guys."

"A likely story!" someone piped up.

"And I'm a virgin!" came another.

Lena looked at Joy, "So malicious." Turning, she quickly went back into her room, locking her door. The others soon followed Lena's lead.

Joy was left standing with the scarf and knife, completely confused. "Guys. I didn't!"

The stranger watched from a distance and smiled.

And so it begins...

TWO

The bike roared over the otherwise quiet countryside. The old couple sitting on the wide wooden porch watched with jaundiced eyes as the bike zoomed full-tilt over the hill in front of their house, sending a cloud of curled, brown leaves twirling before their wise eyes.

"That one will find trouble more sooner than later," the wrinkled, time-worn woman said, reaching with vein knotted hands for her teacup.

The insistent gurgling issuing from his bowels and his wife's comments were the only things keeping her husband from his nap. "Yup," he agreed, hoping to at least stop one of the annoyances. He stared longingly after the bike.

The bike was fast. That is part of the reason why the rider bought it. That and the fact that not many students at a Catholic college would have had the nerve to buy such a big ride. The Indian motorcycle was big enough for two, but today the rider sped down the wide-open roads alone. The sleek black matte beast seemed to absorb the sun, and the owner could feel the power vibrating between denim-clad legs as it raced over the flat roads of Indiana. Fall was in progress, and the warm days were numbered.

Fall was the best time of the year. The trees were on the downside of their colorful peak and the late afternoon sun shimmered yellow-gold through the branches stretched heavenward, seemingly begging God for something. As the bike roared on, everything began to blur.

Feet in vintage snake boots and muscular legs clad in tight denim leggings eased the bike into the next gear. The figure under the black helmet crouched low over the bike's handlebars and smiled at the engine's unrelenting throbbing.

The bike weaved effortlessly in and out of the light traffic, speeding towards Upland. It was good to be away from work for a little while. She'd taken a weekend trip just to unwind before her semi-working vacation. And now she needed to get back home and to her work. It had been so long since she'd been able to relax. Now, she'd be able to relax by starting the renovations and new construction on her childhood home.

She had long since graduated from college and university, but she needed a break. What better way than to party on campus? As part of her weekend trip, she went to campus for an achievement award.

After she celebrated with the faculty, what she found was nothing much had changed for the students. Fall break was upon the *ton*, and last night off-campus had culminated into a drinking party celebrating freedom.

And fornication.

The Indiana University campus was a hotbed. Had she not completed her degrees through distance education programs, she was sure she would have gotten into a lot of trouble on campus. If it had been at St. Mary of the Woods, the rider noted, the nuns would not stand for such tomfoolery.

Not that having sex randomly was her forte, but last night had been ridiculously easy. Maybe it was because she was no longer a student and saw it all for what it was. Or perhaps it was just that she was confident in herself and her success for the first time in her life.

Whatever the reason, she started drinking at Bernie's Beach Bar. It was fun with its indoor/outdoor heated pool and in-pool drink service. And last night was a terrific opportunity to blow off some extra energy that had been building during her company's explosive growth. School and starting a business didn't leave much time for a social life or building relationships. A fact she was sorely aware of through the one serious adult relationship she had tried in her second year of higher education.

What had been even better than the drinking last night were the offers given at the party. One included her former serious boyfriend, Lane Kincaid. He told her he transferred from Indiana State University to Indiana University. The ass actually had the nerve to ask her for sex, "to remember the good part of our relationship." *Well, buddy, it wasn't nearly as good as the offer I accepted last night.*

Remembering the encounter she had finally decided on, the rider smiled again. The man had an angel's face and a whore's heart. They were playing water polo together, and afterward, he said he'd like to give her a "wet pass." Not the most original line, but the tall, dark-haired, blue-eyed man-whore was up for it all. Her wish was his command. Nicole had the feeling she taught the lanky, broad-shouldered man a few things last night that would keep the quality analyst nerd in wet passes for a year.

She stopped the bike at the mom-and-pop gas station close to home. Gas was cheaper outside of small towns, but one of her indulgences was being a patron of local businesses. For most other things, she was extra frugal, and for once if an offer of free sex came in the bargain, so be it. She considered it a benefit and compensation for the hard work she had to put in over the last few years.

She pulled the bike to a stop and flipped the kickstand. Nicole always stopped at the Pump and Go station; it was tradition with her. The owner, Dean Swayne, was a local and always friendly; she'd known him since she was a little girl. And she suspected the man knew better than anyone she needed a kind face during those days. People in service industries like gas stations, hair salons, security, and even personal assistants knew everything about everyone. And Dean Swayne was gregarious, loquacious, and a keen observer of all things human.

Unlocking her gas tank, she pulled off the helmet and let her mass of red hair sweep forward. It felt good to let her head cool off after the ride. She started for the building that was little more than a concrete utility shed with a wooden door.

"Well hello, Nicole Bichey! Back already?" Mr. Swayne, the gnarled owner, greeted her at the door. He always pronounced the name with the correct French flare of a short "I" and "SHAY"

"Have to," she smiled as the man hugged her. He always smelled of horehound candy and cigarettes. "You know how business is." Nicole pulled her heavy backpack off her shoulders for a moment.

Someone her grandmother would have called "a tall drink of water" came from the side of the building. Nodding her head in the direction of the pumps asked, "Who's the new guy? He wasn't here last week."

Mr. Swayne looked out the door to his small business. "I seen a lot of good things you're doing at the old house!" Then harrumphed. "Him. That's Michael Madigan. I guess you could say he's in business, too."

Her heart skipped a beat. Michael. *Keep it together, girl,* she said to herself. "Thanks, it is really coming along." *But many things needed to be changed, cleaned, and removed from the house, too,* she thought.

"What does he do?" Nicole asked, giving Michael another glance. His legs were as scrumptious as she remembered, maybe better. His dark blonde hair glinted in the sun and curled slightly around his ears. She felt a familiar flex between her legs.

Mr. Swayne's lively blue eyes strayed back to Nicole. "Don't you remember him? He graduated up to the high school, oh, about five or six years ago, I'd say. He went to school for a criminal justice degree, and he's been working at the Indiana State Police. In Peru, I think. Still lives in his parent's house down the road a piece. Comes in here just to chat occasionally when he's off duty and ends up doing most of the work, too. I think he's working on something top secret here. But he won't tell me." He wrinkled his nose and, without pausing for breath, slyly commented, "Isn't it time you got one again?"

Nicole's heart didn't flutter with the mention of a boyfriend. She had been over Lane, for some time but hadn't really had time or energy to devote herself to anyone. But her heart skipped a beat at the mention of Michael. And she wasn't blind. Michael Madigan was as beautiful as she remembered him to be.

Nicole gave Mr. Swayne a droll smile,

"Mr. Swayne! You know how busy I am. But," she leaned in, "It never hurts to look around a bit. Just in case." She tilted her head and gave the old man a raffish look. "You can't tell me that you don't still look."

Dean Swayne laughed, holding his hand up. "You got me. Guilty." He lowered his voice, "Personally, I like to think it doesn't matter where you get your appetite, as long as you go home for dinner."

Nicole had to laugh, showing the shallow cleft in her chin. She winked at Mr. Swayne. "How true, how true. Just don't let your wife know about your philosophy. She might disapprove."

Swayne rolled his eyes and held up his arthritis-twisted hand piously, "Don't I know it."

Michael returned and wiped his hands on a towel. "Nice bike. Did you do the custom kit by yourself?"

"Thanks. No, I had it installed," Nicole replied coolly. She could appreciate how perky his pecs were under his fitted t-shirt! Some things did change for the better.

"Of course, you wouldn't need to do it yourself. She's gassed up and ready to go." His gray eyes met her green ones.

Nicole's eyebrows shot up. His attitude bothered her. Why would he say something like that about her? She was about to give him a taste of her razor-sharp tongue but found herself able to put her game face on, "Good, then I guess I will be on my way again." Waving a candy bar and a pack of gum, she asked, "How much?"

"Two eighty."

She dug in her wallet, "And with the fill-up?" Nicole looked at Michael pointedly. Silky, gorgeous hair, even if his demeanor was shitty.

Michael blushed, "Twenty-five thirty-two."

Nicole produced a twenty and six ones. She smiled at Mr. Swayne. "I'll be back soon. I've got a lot of construction to do yet, and as you know, I am expanding." She walked through the old wooden door.

"Nicole, you forgot your change!" Michael called somewhat tauntingly after her.

She turned back and looked at Michael. Boldly she let her eyes rake over him. "Keep it. For your trouble." Flashing another smile, she walked out into the late afternoon sun to her bike.

Nicole clipped her helmet on her black

leather saddlebags. Usually, she wore her helmet because she didn't fancy her brains splattered all over the road, but in the last stretch of highway Nicole loved so much before she got home, Nicole adored the free feeling of the wind on her face and in her hair. Waving goodbye to the pair looking out the window, she headed once again toward Upland.

The two men she left behind looked at her—one with fondness and the other with curiosity. A third figure, outside their view, watched Nicole leave, thinking she needed to be reminded where she came from and where she belonged.

THREE

At the top of the narrow stairway was an old wooden door that led to the attic. On either side of the attic door were doors that led to the two upstairs bedrooms. Nicole grasped the black metal handle on the left door and twisted it.

"Let's just drop our stuff here." Nicole told her friends.

That night Nicole and her slightly older sister, Renee, were having a rare slumber party.

Nicole was the younger, having been born in August and Renee eleven months earlier in September. They were only eleven months apart, and their parents decided to send them to school the same year as they both squeaked in under their September and August birthdays. As a result, they had a group of friends that ranged from 12 to almost 14.

They preferred to go to their friends' homes where they had more freedom from their parents, but this time, they wanted to have all their friends together, and their house was the biggest. Tonight, Lena and Jackie Gammon,

Laurel Bodkins, and Coro Garner made the trek to their home for the most momentous sleepover the sisters ever had.

Renee and Nicole were ashamed of how poor the house looked in comparison to their friends' homes. The shabby farmhouse was comfortable, but almost all the furniture was a hand-me-down mix of blonde pieces from the 1950s and older. Pieces like the 1920s shaving stand and decorated with bright necklaces and scarves or the yellow, rigid plastic, snap-together bookshelves stood out against the fake pine paneling. Beside her bed was a 1950s style bookshelf with tapered legs that doubled as her makeup area. Above the bookshelf hung a large oval mirror with a cheap plastic frame made to look like antique plaster molding.

Not exactly well off despite the fact their father was an engineer, they had taken the old, brown, stained carpet from her father's boss. The pair tried to hide the old and filthy cutouts in the rug for the floor vents by placing furniture over those spots. It made the carpet less tacky, but still, one could see the plywood floor around the room's edge. It didn't help that they attended school with the children of their dad's boss, Bob. If Bob's kids thought anything about it, they never said anything to the girls. And for that, they were grateful.

Still, this room was Nicole's, and she made it as comfortable as possible. She had a ton of books to read, and the best thing was the persistent smell of perfume and makeup, which made her feel more normal compared to her friends.

"So, what are we going to do?" Lena asked, settling on Nicole's bed.

"Well, we can go for a walk." Renee suggested.

"To where? There isn't anything around here." Lena complained.

"Yeah, there's no boys," her sister, Jackie, chimed in, tossing her sleeping bag on the floor.

"We can't watch movies till my parents go to bed. We only get dial-up out here, so streaming doesn't work," Renee explained.

"We could play basketball," Nicole suggested.

"That's for me!" Laurel declared. She was the center on the Eastbrook Junior High School team.

"Sounds good," Coro emphatically agreed. "It will be good to get outside and do something active. I need to practice my lay-ups."

Reluctantly, the others agreed, and they walked the two acres to the barn, where the basketball hoop was located. For the time being, the issue of the country setting and boys was forgotten.

The rest of the night, the girls ate pizza from a local restaurant, Art's, and popped popcorn, drizzling it with butter and cheese. They eagerly watched moves on the television downstairs with DVDs they chose a week ago and had the rental company mail to them. They enjoyed watching movies that scared them, including one called "Maniac", about a man who killed women and turned them into mannequins which later turned on him.

When the girls decided to sleep, they found it much too warm upstairs. Even with the window air conditioning unit, the room was stifling with so many warm bodies.

Only Renee and Jackie stayed upstairs in Nicole's somewhat now less humid room. The girls were close, and they would rather stay together than with the rest of the girls anyway.

The other girls retired to the room used as a one-room schoolhouse in the late 1800s. It had a fireplace that was most definitely not in use. It had a huge window air conditioning unit that did a good job keeping the humidity down in the house, and it kept that room particularly cold.

Sometime in the middle of the night, the friendship of the girls would change forever.

FOUR

Now that she was just shy of nine months away from graduating from Eastbrook High School, it was harder for Nicole's parents to control her. Not that she had many social offers. Since that fated sleepover, her social life was a bit stifled. The girls talked to her now more than a couple of years ago, but just barely. She had casual friends, but they didn't do anything outside of class. The offers she did have were summarily denied if they were not from Catholic people.

Today, Nicole grabbed her bicycle and navigated her way to the pond about a few miles from her house. She often spent time there reading, writing, or just trying to stay out of her parents' way.

One feature about the area they lived in was the surfeit of small, natural, spring-fed ponds. At one time, the region had been a mecca for people seeking natural cures from spring water. Nicole chose one further away from her house and not close to the road to spend more time away from her parents. They thought she was riding her bike on the low-traffic country roads. Nicole was actually spending a far more enjoyable time reading and doing a little writing.

Nicole was perspiring and warm on the sunny, clear day, and she decided to go swimming. She stripped to her boyshorts and bra, plunging into the cool, semi-shaded water. Nicole felt vaguely decadent. If her parents knew she was parading around in her underwear, she had no doubt she would be beaten within an inch of her life.

They controlled her life from dawn to dusk. They censored the people she was with, colored her views on sex, and imposed her consciousness with extreme religious beliefs. Okay, her mother more than her father, but showing skin was not on their agenda with either parent.

Luckily they did not restrict what she read, and voraciously, she read, finding the real world outside her parents' inconsistent warped view.

Today, the water felt so good on her skin, and she began to float lazily after a while. A voice broke into her thoughts.

"What are you doing here?" a masculine voice asked.

In her half-clothed state, Nicole had stopped floating and instantly covered her body with the water. Sputtering, she asked, "What are you doing here?"

The tall young man sardonically smiled, "My parents own this pond."

"Oh," was all Nicole was able to manage.

"Do you normally trespass on other people's property and skinny dip?"

Nicole's green eyes blazed at his insolent attitude, and she found her voice. Yes, it was not her property, but she wasn't desecrating it, for God's sake! And she wasn't even naked. "Only when I think I can get away with it." She glared at him, "Do you think you could turn your back so I can get out?"

Leisurely, the young man sat down at the water's edge and spoke to her. "Now, that all depends. It seems that you took a swim, trespassed on my property—"

"Your parents' property," Nicole corrected tartly.

"And I don't know if they would like that," he finished, ignoring her jibe.

"I've never hurt anything, nor have I ever seen anyone else here."

"But the kids go to the bridge next to

my parents' property and destroy parts of the woods there. How do I know you won't bring a bunch of your friends back here to party?" He reached in his pocket and pulled out a piece of gum.

"I am not them. And besides, why would I do something stupid like that? I've been coming here for several years." Damn, but she was tired of dog paddling. The only alternative was going in the shallow end and leaving herself vulnerable to this sniveling idiot. "I come here for quiet, not for partying."

"But I don't know that." He popped the gum in his mouth and began chewing. He seemed to think for a moment, "I'll tell you what. We can make a deal. I'll let you swim here—"

"In exchange for what?" Nicole wasn't that naive.

He smiled. "In exchange for a kiss."

Nicole couldn't believe her ears. "Wait a minute. In exchange for a kiss, one kiss, you won't be bothered that I come here alone sometimes."

"Yes."

"How do I know you won't bother me from now on?"

"I guess you'll have to trust me." His eyes twinkled.

"Turn around and let me get dressed first."

Again, the stranger-owner's son smiled. "Kiss me. Now." He held out his arms.

She didn't want to come out in her underwear. Nicole wasn't ashamed of her body, but she had enough of her parents' influence that made her feel like she was naked. But Nicole wasn't going to be cowed by this person. "Sure, be right out," she called with more confidence than she felt. Nicole began walking to the shore.

She had only walked two or three steps when a dark blonde man's sardonic smile faded, 'No, wait— that isn't what— hold on!" He jumped up, turned, and grabbed her towel. Without bothering to take off his dusty boots, he waded into the water, and effortlessly dog paddled to her with her towel.

"Put this around you. I was only joking." His dark blonde hair fell over his ruddy face. His ash gray eyes seemed repentant.

Nicole wrapped the towel around her, surprised by his chivalry, and continued to walk to shore.

For the first time, Nicole noticed that

he looked absolutely absurd, dripping water from his wavy blond hair and his heavy boots oozing. A piece of algae clung to his chin, and Nicole suppressed an urge to laugh, biting her lip slightly.

"I was only kidding," he iterated again, stumbling lamely.

"That's a shame," Nicole boldly stated, surprising herself. She didn't want to be mauled, but she couldn't help wondering what a kiss would be like from this handsome person.

Staring at each other for what seemed like forever, they came together in a breathtaking single kiss. Short but warm and soft. This was not the kiss of a monster, just an awkward young man kissing an equally awkward eighteen-year-old who had never been kissed before.

When they parted, they both colored slightly.

"Look, you can come here anytime. I won't bother you. I'm sorry. I don't know what came over me. You looked like you were having fun, and you're so pretty…"

Nicole tilted her head, "You aren't so bad yourself. Maybe we'll see each other again sometime."

FIVE

After the day she met the tall, blond stranger, Nicole spent even more time at the pond. Her mystery man with incredible gray eyes turned out to be Michael Madigan. They spent their time together talking about their hopes and dreams. He wanted to be a detective.

She told him of her dreams to get away from her parents, help people, do something useful, and be self-sufficient. "I want to write and work with technology. Maybe combine the two."

They also talked about other things, including the hauntings in her house. Nicole told Michael about what happened to Lena. At first, he didn't believe Nicole. But from the bodiless boots to the children playing chess to the fact that Nicole and Renee had seen other spirits in the house, Michael was soon converted.

The last time she saw Michael before she went to college was right after her parents' funeral.

"Honestly, I had hoped your parents' case would be more challenging." Michael turned to face her.

They were lying under a weeping willow tree-shaded from the early summer sun. Michael was shirtless and in shorts, which was typical for him. Often they liked to lay in the sun and work on their tans.

Michael brought a picnic lunch and a large blanket as he routinely did. The food was from his mother's kitchen. Michael was raised much differently. The people in his family were open and cared deeply for each other. The family lived their lives trying to be good people. His father worked as a farmer and volunteer fireman for many years. However, shortly after Nicole and Michael met, his dad died of a heart attack.

She comforted him during the aftermath. "Your mom needs you." She told him. "If you can't meet, I understand." But Michael showed up every Saturday.

Although her parents tried to control her every move, her parents weren't smart enough to track internet usage. Nicole had a burner account that she would send e-mails from. She was sure to log out, not remember the account, and clear her browsing history.

Neither of them cared about their parents knowing about their friendship for different reasons. Nicole because her parents would end it as a control issue as Michael was not Catholic. Michael didn't advertise their relationship because his mother had more things on her mind. One was trying to keep their home. She rented the fields, but it was a struggle.

Nicole ate a chicken wing. His mother was a terrific cook. She eyed the feast before them; fried chicken, potato salad, baked beans, and fresh peach pie. "Does she ever say anything about you taking so much food for picnics?"

"No, she knows I have an appetite."

Getting back to their conversation, Nicole raised her eyebrows. "I struggle to wish I felt more, but because of the people they were, I can't. I wish my sister could have talked to me. But we weren't raised to ask for help- or feel much empathy for others."

Michael shook his head, "I don't believe that. I can tell by talking with you that you feel. Deeply." He kissed her.

Nicole returned the kiss, loving the feel of his arms around her. He made her feel safe, warm and at least cared for.

Michael's hand slipped over her tank and under it as his hand had traveled so many times before. His mouth replaced his hands, and he sprung the front clasp of her bra and freed her beautiful, firm breasts.

The food was forgotten. Michael's tongue made insistent kisses over her nipples, his teeth nipping gently at the berry tips. Nicole threw her head back at the exquisite sensation and gave a tiny mew.

Michael moved his head down and snaked his slightly calloused hands beneath her shirt, pushing it up towards her neck. Nicole helped by sitting up and pulling it the rest of the way off.

She was a little embarrassed to have him see her, finally, partially naked. He'd seen her in underwear on their first meeting, and it had been months since that time. They hadn't done anything remotely close to this until recently.

Nicole had gone on many walks during the winter and met him at the utility shed, not too far from the pond. In the comfort of a closed space, they spent time using a wood-burning stove and chatting while her mother and father thought she'd gone on a walk.

Michael's cock was rock hard, but he wanted to take it slowly. Nicole was so beautiful with her clothes on, and to see her even partially unclothed came close to unmanning him. They both knew the other hadn't had sex before.

"I bought some protection," Michael said, pulling out a handful of condoms from his pocket.

Nicole nodded. Although they were virgins, they wanted to be safe from disease and a baby. She stood and pulled her capri jeans and panties down, revealing her muscular legs achieved by so much bike riding and the place that had been hers alone until now. Stepping out of the pool of clothing, she stood before Michael, completely naked. Nicole resisted the urge to cover herself.

Michael's mouth went dry at the beautiful sight of the gorgeous young woman before him. He stood as well and looked intently at her as he stripped his shorts and boxers off. The shade highlighted tanned arms, chest, and legs against his groin's stark whiteness and the length showcased there. He kissed her again, pressing his body against hers.

Nicole could feel the two of them trembling as they kissed. She knew he was nervous, and that made her feel better about her own nervousness.

Their kiss deepened, and Nicole felt herself go wet between her legs. Unconsciously she pressed her legs together to alleviate the throbbing she felt. Michael's hands slid gently down her bare, soft back and sank to his knees. Nicole was embarrassed to have him so close to the wetness she felt. She moved to step away.

"No, stay," he whispered against her curvy stomach, cupping her buttocks. He breathed her scent in, a heady combination of sunshine, sweat, and her. He looked at the V where her legs met her mons and ran a finger lightly in the juncture. Michael felt how excited Nicole was.

"I'm sorry..." she began.

"Why?" He looked up.

"It's, uh, a bit messy."

Michael opened her lips with two fingers and kissed the button he found there. "I should hope so." He smiled up at her.

Nicole almost fell over as Michael replaced his lips with his tongue. The bright starred explosion she felt behind her eyes made her weak, and Michael held her firmly with his forearm across her soft rounded ass cheeks.

"Move your legs a little apart. That's it." His voice was muffled with his mouth planted firmly between Nicole's legs. He reached up and gently stroked her breasts. He replaced his mouth with two fingers, pulling and gently twisting her elongated clitoris as he gently rubbed her nipples. He looked up at her, his mouth glistening with her juices, "I can't make any promises about quality. This is new to me, too."

Nicole gasped, trying to comprehend what she was feeling. Michael's touch was so arousing. She didn't care about quality or anything else. She felt like she just wanted him inside her. Kneeling with Michael, she said, "Let me touch you, too." She moved forward, and as Michael leaned back on his elbows, they laughed as her necklace got caught around his penis.

She ran her hand over his chest, feeling the silky hair. Nicole rubbed her face against his tummy and looked at the beckoning arrow of hair that led down to his gorgeous penis. Nicole may not have had any experience with them, but she and her girlfriends had certainly looked in their parents' sock drawers and online. She touched his hard cock, reveling in how warm it was. His hairy balls were taut, and a little liquid came out the tip of his shaft. Nicole squeezed his penis, and it twitched, more liquid seeping out and over his soft tip.

Nicole could smell the musky sweetness of his sex. She licked her lips and ran her mouth over the top of his cock. He was salty, sweet, and tasted so good.

He sat up suddenly, "As much as I like that and have dreamed about this, if you don't stop, we'll be done before we get there." Michael kissed Nicole insistently, rolling her on her back. He paused and fumbled briefly with the condom and got it rolled down.

Nicole opened her legs, inviting him in. He rubbed his penis over her lips and clitoris, and Nicole thought she would go crazy with wanting. She never knew it would be like this. He looked at her questioningly as if asking for one last permission before proceeding.

Nicole kissed her answer to Michael. She ran her hands down his back and his buttocks to help him push in. He worked himself in and then out until a white-hot flash of light seared her mind and Nicole breathed in sharply. She heard their breath coming raggedly, he trying to maintain and she trying to absorb the slash of pain and the satisfying feel of him inside her. Her legs wrapped around his waist.

There, in the shade of the great oak tree, their lunch long forgotten, they made love the entire afternoon, discovering each other and delighting in the response of the other. They stayed far longer than they should have but didn't stop until every last condom had been used.

SIX

For late April, the weather was gorgeous. The buds on the trees were about to explode with the riot of leaves they provided every year. With the sun out, the temperature felt warmer than the 55 degrees predicted for the day. The birds chirped loudly as the girls drove home.

People were out working in their yards.

It was now the weekend, and life was good.

"What is going on?" Nicole asked Renee as they turned into the driveway. They saw the police cars before Renee turned the late model Chevy Malibu station wagon into the gravel path.

"Miss Bichey? MISS BICHEY?" A deputy walked quickly along the passenger's side of the moving car.

Renee stopped and rolled the window down next to Nicole. "Yes, officer? What's going on?" Nicole asked.

The young red-headed deputy put his hands on the car. "I need you both to get out of the car and come with me."

As they exited the car, the deputy asked

them both to accompany him to a group of police officers.

"What do you think they want?" Renee whispered.

"I don't know. Probably Mom and Dad finally got caught doing something illegal. Maybe Mom played beat the bank too many times with checks."

Renee snorted and whispered, "All these cops for that?"

Sheriff Rutledge approached the trio. He motioned for them to sit in the back of the ambulance. Sitting together, Sheriff Rutledge squatted in front of them. "Girls, I have something to tell you that you may find difficult."

Nicole's gaze drifted to the door of the house. A stretcher with a sheet draped body emerged. She glanced back to the sheriff.

Sheriff Rutledge glanced back and sighed. "I told them to wait," he muttered. Looking back at the girls, he simply said, "Your parents are dead. Both of them."

The silence seemed to intensify everything around Nicole. She heard the birds sing more loudly, and a lone woodpecker knocked the deadwood nearby so loudly, Nicole felt a growing pressure.

Then suddenly, Nicole felt free, and immediately, she felt remorse.

"W-what happened to them?" Renee was saying.

"They were shot. That's all you need to know."

Nicole spoke. "Do you know who did it?"

Sheriff Rutledge wiped his balding head with a bandana. "Not yet. The Carters across the way heard yelling and heard the shots. But the murderer left some clues."

"Clues?" Renee questioned.

"We don't want to release that information yet. I've probably told you too much. We're going to take you down to the station and have someone stay with you tonight. We'll get in touch with your family and get you some help."

SEVEN

The aftermath of her parent's murder was a nightmare. Renee and Nicole were adults, so there was no recourse within the Child Protective Services. None of their family members offered to help them or take them in. Many of them never even replied to inquiries. Their neighbors, Fay and Joseph Gutzwiller, offered to take care of them. The couple had experience with a horrific death of their own. Their son, Charles, died when he was young. It was something the couple never recovered from.

"Oh, here they come." Fay said. Their dogs barked, confirming the arrival of Nicole and Renee. "M.J. and Lady, stop that!"

Over the years, they would wave to the girls and send them cookies. Their parents would often either eat the treats themselves or pitch them immediately into the trash, calling the Gutzwillers "fucking do-gooders".

"Do you want more to eat?" Fay asked the girls. She'd made pot roast with potatoes and carrots.

"No, thank you," they said. The portions

were outrageous, and the food tasted so good. Nicole felt terrible as they were feeding them so well. And it had to be costing them a small fortune.

She'd tried to broach the subject once, and they said it was no trouble, but Nicole and Renee could appreciate the time that went into the food. Her chili was full of meat and beans and thick, not like their mother's chili that was more water than substance.

And the laundry. Fay Gutzwiller was a homemaker and took this role as her genuine job. Fresh, clean laundry included crisp, ironed sheets, towels, and clothes. Even the girls' skirts were meticulously fastened to hangers with safety pins.

Renee and Nicole agreed living with the Gutzwillers was the best they'd ever experienced living. Warm beds, plenty to eat, and the Gutzwillers didn't make them feel like they owed them anything or that they were in the way.

Renee never seemed happier to Nicole. Before her parents died, she tried to date a guy, Jeremy Charrier, but her parents put the kibosh on that, citing that they didn't like him. Which just drew the young pair closer and fostered a determination to be together. Nicole knew they were secretly meeting, but it was an unspoken pact. They didn't question where the other went or who they went with. Now, with Lindsey and Dee gone, she was able to see Jeremy regularly.

After Renee was arrested, the Gutzwillers continued to shepherd Nicole. They would have continued to support Renee more than they did, who the couple considered a lost child, but just like Nicole, who was a relative, they could not visit her. Still, they did send her money and notes about themselves and Nicole. They felt it their duty to help as God would have. They helped Nicole decide how to move forward for her immediate future. They encouraged her to keep her plans to go to college and got her into an earlier start session at St. Mary of the Woods College. They also helped negotiate her parents' estate.

Currently, Nicole sat with Mae Davidson, her parent's insurance agent. Nicole remembered going to see Mae when she was very young. Her mother mainly visited her and seemed to take forever to get anything done. Mae had always been a businesswoman. She graduated high school and started work as a secretary, working her way into insurance when her male counterparts had problems working with emotional widows. Proving herself outside of death claims, she built her knowledge and business.

Her office, a former dress shop, had a wide-open feel with different waiting areas, snacking, and relaxing. Even her personal assistant had a spot in the space.

Mae met her husband, Jack, later in life, and they never had children. He breezed in and out occasionally, and when he did, he was careful not to disturb her. He had several business ventures of his own.

Mae was tough as nails, but she was a traditional wife at heart. She closed promptly at 4:30 to drive the ten minutes home to have a home-cooked dinner for her husband every night. In fact, Mae would even go home on her lunch hour to start the sumptuous meals like pot roast, roasted chicken, and other meals that took forever to cook. "A crockpot is a lazy cook's tool," she was fond of saying.

Nicole couldn't believe what she heard from Mae Davidson.

"Your parents had a lot of life insurance. They had made the change to up the amount shortly before they died. I never quite understood why." She pulled the paperwork out and looked over her black bifocals. "But you get the benefit of that decision. They had two million dollars between them. I told them it was not necessary. There were times they needed that premium money for other bills. But," she sighed, "that doesn't matter now."

Maybe it was their mutual contract so that neither of them did the other in. Nicole shuddered at the morbid thought.

"Since they were each other's beneficiaries and obviously cannot collect and your sister is ineligible for any part of the money, it is yours as soon as we file the papers with the insurance company." Mae looked at Nicole again over her glasses, somewhat disapprovingly, "What you do with it afterward is up to you."

Nicole was shocked. She had more money than she ever dreamed.

Mae continued, "I would suggest a good financial planner. If you don't have one, I can certainly recommend one."

As if she wanted anyone who did business with her parents to give her advice.

"No, thank you. I have one." She lied, but she knew the Gutzwillers could help with that.

When the paperwork was finished and the information was electronically sent to the insurance company, Mae looked hard at Nicole, "Just remember, we reap what we sow."

Nicole picked up the paperwork. She did not have to answer to this woman. "No one knows that more than I do or my parents."

EIGHT

The heavy doors slammed shut behind her. This was not where Nicole wanted to be. Nicole walked with two female guards through a small, dimly lit walkway between outer cell doors and the limestone building with its barred windows. An inside cell block with an additional locked, barred door lay behind the exterior doors. The whole area smelled of urine, sweat, and desperation.

The assault on her nose was nothing compared to the glimpse of prisoners Nicole saw. The jail was small; each cell had four women in a ten by ten space. The metal bunk beds attached to the thin walls framed the small sink and seatless toilet, which graced the only open wall space. At the bottom of the wall under the sink was a small electric heater, which seemed a futile attempt to heat the dark, damp area.

"Wait here," one of the female guards barked, stepping behind Nicole. With her long blonde hair in a bun, the other walked from the group and down into the cells.

"Bichey," she called, pronouncing it

"bitchy", "You've got a visitor."

In her jail-issued orange shirt and pocketless denim pants, Renee shuffled slowly towards Nicole, her feet in chains. Her hands were in front of her, wedged together with zip ties. An orange sweatshirt was draped over her shoulders. Her hair, which generally sat at the middle of her back now, was shoulder length.

"Ok, sit," the bun guard said. She pushed Renee onto the bench.

The pair looked at one another.

Finally, Renee spoke. "So, what do you think of the new digs?" Renee broke into a smile.

Nicole had started school the day after Renee was convicted. Although she was doing classes from home, she was swamped trying to get a sound footing in her classes. Today was the first day she saw Renee since the police arrested her, and the memory of that day was as fresh in her mind as if it had only happened a few hours ago.

When the police showed up a month after the funeral, the good times with the Gutzwillers came crashing down hard. The police found the gun at the house the day of the murder. It had Renee's fingerprints on it, although Nicole attested they were not allowed to touch the weapon.

Additionally, the police questioned many people about Renee's whereabouts during the murder, pinpointed between 1:30 p.m. and 3 p.m. They were told by many teachers she had been seen throughout the day, making it difficult to believe she had done it. Renee was charged with first-degree murder.

Renee displayed a lot of anger after her arrest. First, she was angry when they took her away and became unable to control herself in jail. As a result, the court did not believe Renee was competent to stand trial. When she was evaluated at the Indiana Women's State Prison, the psychologists diagnosed her with having a severe case of psychopathy. Renee showed no remorse for her crime. She showed no signs of empathy, and she clearly demonstrated she did not know the difference between right and wrong. For now, she remained at the local jail but would be transferred back to the psychiatric ward until a time she could stand trial if that time ever came.

"Seems a bit uncomfortable, to be honest. Is there anything you need?" Nicole asked, not really knowing what she was doing there, nor what to do for this person who killed her parents. Her parents sucked, but killing was wrong.

"I have everything I need for now. When I get transferred to the hospital, they will provide everything I am entitled to." Renee gestured to her attire. "Not much to look at, but easy to get ready in the morning."

"I still don't know how you did it."

Renee smiled malevolently, "I had my ways."

"I am sorry you are here," Nicole said slowly.

Renee dismissed the gesture, "Don't be. They deserved it. Our parents were the worst human beings on the face of this pathetic earth. They never wanted us. They didn't even want each other unless it benefited them in some way." Renee snorted, "What I did was something they would have done themselves if they'd had a shred of integrity."

"Mom and dad were shitty parents, but it was about to end for us. We are eighteen. I was already there and ready to make my move out to college- even if it meant working my ass off 24/7. You could have made a plan, too." Nicole leaned forward. "Who else deserves it? What are your criteria for making that decision? If you ever hope to get out, you better figure it out."

Renee chuckled, "You of all people should know the answer to your own question. I ain't never getting out of here. I will go to the hospital, and they will stick pins in me to see what makes me tick. If they ever think I am sane, I will be in prison forever."

"But what about living? What about Jeremy? Doing something outside what Mom and Dad guided for us. They were inconsistent and selfish with their own demons. You were so close."

Renee moved her head from side to side. "I couldn't take it anymore. They weren't going to pay for college. They wouldn't give us access to their taxes for financial aid. They tried to make me stop seeing Jeremy. I hated them. Fuck horrible people." She snorted, "And Jeremy. It seems he's been too busy to write. What a disappointment!"

"I can talk to him..."

"Don't waste your time."

Nicole felt helpless. "I want to put some money in an account for you."

Renee nodded, "That would be nice. The

Gutzwillers have, too. They were so good to us, though Charles was a mean kid. It will make the transition easier. Thank you."

"I–I will miss you."

Renee gave a nod, "Live your life. Come and see me if and when they let you. Now, let's not get sticky. That's not our family."

Renee called out to the bun guard, who was positioned behind her, "I'm ready to go."

She turned back to Nicole, flashing a wintery smile, "Till we meet again." Renee gave a jaunty wink and walked away.

NINE

Nicole enjoyed attending school through St. Mary of the Woods College, but she hated taking classes on campus. The grounds were gorgeous with wooded trails, shady green spaces, and creepy old buildings. It reminded her of the ghoulishness of her own home. Her program was a distance education program, but some classes could be knocked out in three days. Taking such a short amount of time to complete a course and get credit was phenomenal.

But it was the superficiality and snide remarks. Many people at her high school were the same. Being a small community and having weird parents was one thing. Having a sister in a psychiatric hospital for the murder of those parents made national news put a whole new light on snarky.

And if her parents ever thought she was loose, they would be rolling in their graves at how much fornication went on here. Although the student code of conduct forbade anything to put the students on "perilous footing of their mortal soul", so much went on behind closed doors.

The women at school had been exceedingly snotty for the most part, especially when it came to money and looks. Looks, she knew could be compensated for with personality and other attributes. Not that she had any problems with her mass of red hair and green eyes. Her nice pair of tits didn't hurt either. And her body, though not that of a model, seemed to attract the men. Who knew they were interested in a woman with a little extra?

Not that she took a lot of men up on their offers. Nicole was much too focused to stray too much. She turned into the cemetery to finish her lap around campus before lunch break was over.

The women assumed she was poor because she didn't live on campus. They did not know about her money because she didn't disclose it. Just this week, someone made a remark about the clothes she wore. Nicole packed jeans, T-shirts, and sweatshirts. She wanted to be comfortable while in class. The girl, Lisa, said, "It must be nice to be able to be so casual in your clothing choices."

Nicole turned to her and said, "I'm fearless that way. The difference between us is that I can change my clothes and still feel good about myself. No matter what, you'll always be a knock-off influencer wannabe."

The look on her face was worth the price of tuition. Lisa's mouth opened and closed like a fish, and Nicole couldn't resist adding, "Close your mouth and give it a welcome rest." After she said it, she desperately hoped they would not be required to do group work in the class.

Which was not her luck. After lunch, they returned to their class and were paired together. Lisa started complaining about splitting the work and how Nicole did her part. Nicole was about to say something when Lisa asked to be excused to go to the bathroom. Shortly after she left, the class heard a horrible crash and found Lisa unconscious at the foot of the broad stairway. She swore she was pushed, but no one was around.

After class, Nicole walked back toward her temporary dorm room. She crossed the main road and headed to the shady back entrance of Guerin Hall.

"Hey, Nicole!"

Nicole turned to see who was calling her. To her surprise, she was face to face with Lena. Even Lena, who she had been friends with in junior high school, was as duplicitous as the rest.

"Hi, Lena." Nicole said coolly, not wanting another confrontation that day, "What's up?"

Lena stopped her bike and put her feet on the pavement. "Not much, just surprised to see you on campus. I thought you were in the external program."

"I am. But I am here for a few days to knock out a class."

"Oh, yes, you are practically legendary around here. You're on track to finish your degree in a couple years versus four?"

Nicole regarded Lena with a smile, "Yes, that's correct."

Lena smiled wolfishly, "Of course, you'd want to get back to Renee. How is she, by the way?"

Nicole tilted her head, "Why is it again you want to know? You've not spoken with her or me, for that matter, for a long time."

Lena kept her smile in place, "I went out with Jeremy Charrier the other night. He said she's in a prison hospital for crazy people." Lena's eyes glittered, "How hard that must be for you."

Nicole disliked Lena intensely at that

moment. She couldn't believe they had ever been friends. And Jeremy wasn't much better. She tried to talk to him after visiting Renee, but he just said it was too hard. Now, he was some sort of occult guru and probably another notch on Lena's shattered chastity belt.

She moved closer to Lena and pulled her long black hair back. She whispered, "Judging from you never being on the Dean's list, I suspect you've had to blow your way into your position at the school. Much like I suspect, you got your high school diploma. So don't think anything you have to say about my family matters. I would suggest you confine your concern to how you'll find enough tricks to pay for school. Because you do not want to fuck with me." She shoved Lena's head away from her.

Lena's head was unnaturally cocked, and her eyes were wide with surprise. "We all know how fucked up your house was and your family. Like father, like daughter."

Nicole snorted, "No more fucked up than you were. Did you drive your parents to an early grave?" Nicole let go of Lena's hair and pushed her away. "I'd get out of here before I report you for behavior unbecoming of a St. Mary of the Woods student. I am sure Mother

Superior would love to hear about your dates with Jeremy and the myriad of other men that parade through your sheets."

Pushing her hair back into place, Lena left in a huff.

"That's telling her. Fucking bitch."

Nicole turned around to see who said the words, but she was alone.

TEN

"Oooh, she pisses me off!"

Jeremy was hunkered down in the bed, enjoying the after-shocks pulsing through his cock. Lena was good in bed, but her ranting was killing his buzz. He'd been able to get her mind temporarily off of it by distracting her into bed.

"Don't worry about her. She is nothing in comparison with you." He tried to short circuit the pending blowup.

"She thinks she is so great just because she is finishing school early. Dean's list. The darling of the faculty." Lena's naked body was quivering with rage.

Jeremy looked at her dusky nipples standing at attention, and he grazed them with his lips. Anything to get her off the subject of the Bichey family. "Nicole Bichey is a drudge. All she does is study and network. You, on the other hand…"

Lena pulled herself away from Jeremy. "She is a freak. Her family was a bunch of freaks, and the house Nicole lived in is just wrong. And yet, she gets all the attention. The faculty doesn't even notice me."

Jeremy looked quizzically at Lena, "What does her house have to do with anything? Why does the faculty need to notice you?"

Lena sighed, "You wouldn't understand.

"Probably not."

"She came from the same background, but she has always put herself above everyone in grades, attitude... And her parents weren't anything special. The stories I could tell you!"

Jeremy chuckled, "I am sure you could."

"And her house is haunted as fuck!"

"Haunted?"

"After seeing what I saw there, I spent one night there and never went back."

Liar, Jeremy smiled. He knew better. "Tell me about it."

Lena told him about the ghost that had changed her life, and it intrigued Jeremy.

"Perhaps there are some things we can do to get back at Nicole for you." Jeremy wouldn't mind an opportunity to see Nicole. She visited him after her sister's conviction, and Jeremy was surprised at how good she looked. And she had money. At least that is what the rumor said. The only thing Lena had going is her hot body. "But for now, I know there is one thing

I do understand about you better than anyone and that that's what gets you off."

She sighed as she felt his mouth between the warm folds of her wet lips, "Yes, I suppose you do. But seriously, what are we going to do about her?"

Jeremy raised his head up, "Whatever you want, my beautiful cock-slut. Maybe we should scare her into submission. Using your ghost."

Lena smiled at the thought, "Maybe we should." She rolled Jeremy over onto his back, and in a rare exhibition of giving, she wrapped her moist mouth around his penis. *Yes*, she thought, *scaring that bitch could be the highlight of her year.*

"That's it, take it all in. Tell me how you like it."

Lena moaned, "I love sucking your cock, daddy."

Jeremy smiled to himself. *I know you do.*

The figure looking down from the attic space was livid. They deserved each other and to be taught a lesson.

The next day Lena was sent to the Dean's office. Dean Joyce Simmons sat behind a large desk. Several faculty, nuns, and priests were seated in chairs to her right.

"Please sit." She motioned for Lena to take a seat in front of her. "It's come to our attention you've broken the school conduct code."

"I don't know what you mean." Lena lied.

"A young man was seen leaving your dorm room about three in the morning."

"It couldn't have been my room." Lena tried to convince the Dean.

"The security cameras picked it up." The Dean cut her off. "Do you still deny it? Is there an extenuating circumstance?"

Lena was not the quickest thinker. "No, I guess not."

The Dean sat back, "Alright, then we have to choose how to fix this situation. We could dismiss you," she paused for effect.

Lena gasped.

"But we would hate to do that." Dean Simmons continued, "Father Branigan?"

Lena was sure Nicole was behind this. She would get even with that bitch if it was the last thing she did.

ELEVEN

When Nicole graduated from St. Mary of the Woods College, the fanfare was just too much. Sitting in the small music conservatory hall, roughly the size of an old theater, it embarrassed Nicole.

"The next graduate came into this program and broke all records. Summa cum laude, Dean's list for every semester she's been a student and a graduate in our external degree program after only eighteen months." The director of the program, Miss Anne Brooke, was eager to speak about a person who had been instrumental in helping market the same program she was in and grow the number of participants over the last few months.

"This graduate was motivated and served as a face to the external degree program and mentor to new enrollees. Given what had happened to her parents, Anne was surprised but pleased with the response.

"In addition, during that time, she networked with a variety of our alumni and is well on her way to becoming a force in adult education. Graduating today as valedictorian with her bachelor's of science in digital media communications, starting her adult education master's program tomorrow, Nicole Bichey!"

Despite her dislike of being recognized, she preferred to say in the shadows. Nicole took a deep breath and stepped forward to receive her well-earned diploma. She heard the Gutzwillers cheer for her, and Nicole allowed herself a small smile.

That was a year ago.

Today, sitting in the mass auditorium, Nicole felt a great sense of accomplishment. She completed her bachelor's degree in eighteen months due to a combination of applied professional credit, a great deal of CLEP exams, and AP credit from high school. She completed her master's in a year and was now waiting to receive her diploma. This was certainly one to write about in the alumni magazines.

"What an inspiration our special guest speaker and soon-to-be-graduate of the School of Education is! Not only did she finish her bachelor's degree in record time, but she also completed her master's in Adult Education in one year. Summa cum laude. And," the Dean went on, "Has one of the fastest-growing adult education consultancies in the United States,

Learning Tide. With no further ado, I present the most distinguished, Nicole Bichey!"

Nicole rose to the podium and began, "Thank you, Dean. Distinguished faculty, my mentors," she nodded to the two professors who had helped her so much, "and all the parents and my peers.

"I started this journey long before my parents' deaths. I began it by learning to adapt when they did not love me. I learned to listen for their triggers, signaling an impending explosion. And," she paused for emphasis, "I learned to overcome."

Nicole grabbed the mic and moved from behind the stand. "You might think this is a sad tale, and it is, but no more sad than anything else you've dealt with." She raised her hand and pointed out to the audience. "The circumstances may be different for all of you. Death, disappointment, regret," she ticked them off on her fingers, "But the result is the same. We are here. We have completed our degrees, and we are ready to join the world to make our marks."

She moved down the stairs to the masses. "How many of you thought you'd never get here. Show of hands." Nicole raised hers in solidarity. "I didn't. Not at first. Not even after I finished my bachelor's degree. I didn't think I was worthy. And a master's degree." Rolling her eyes heavenward, she continued, "No, no, I am the first in my family to finish a master's degree.

"It doesn't matter what lies you told yourself you didn't believe them. I wanted to prove to myself I could do this. I wanted to rise above the abusive parents, their unfortunate deaths- yes, they were horrible parents, but they didn't deserve to die that way. I believed in myself. I graduated." She moved through the aisles, "I graduated, and I started my life's work. I did the work. I asked for help. I accepted the advice, even when it was difficult. I called and networked and took rejection and the wins. And I always have a Plan A through Z."

She looked at all the graduates and parents. They were mesmerized. While she was most definitely an extroverted introvert, she found she was skilled at bringing a rapport out in a group. Nicole brought it all home.

"And that is what I challenge you to do. You've done a ton of work, to be sure. And you might be exhausted from it or tomorrow from the serious partying you're about to do," Another wave of laughter erupted.

"I challenge you to never stop working for what you want. Whether you find your profession to be what you stick with your whole life or whether you work to do something else. Even if it is a hobby. Do the work and watch the rewards appear for you to reap. As a successful businesswoman once told me, 'you reap what you sow,' and I challenge you to do the work and harvest a bounty of good your whole life through."

She paused as the crowd went wild. Nicole colored slightly. She was never quite at ease being front and center. It was something she had to learn quickly to manage. Out of panic, if nothing else, in the earlier days of her business.

She started waving her hands to calm them down. "With the indulgence of the school for just a few more minutes. I have a surprise for you and them. I am so grateful for the start I got. After my parents died, the Gutzwiller's," She motioned to her neighbors who had taken such good care of her, "took me under their wing. They never asked for anything in return. The one thing I want to tell them, aside from any honors I've received, is to thank you.

Thank you for helping me, believing in me, and helping me to see my worth." Nicole teared up and ran to give the couple a hug. A thunderous round of applause took minutes to die down.

"Alright, alright. Let's get out of this sticky situation. Now, the surprises for you. I am incredibly grateful for the guidance I have had. I am so fortunate to go to school and not worry about where my tuition was coming from. So I want to give back to my peers, their parents for believing in them, and the school for believing in us."

She hopped back up to the stage and sat down on the edge. Nicole was in her element when she was just one of the crowd and not a stuffy, scared to mingle speaker.

"Let me explain how this works. Under two chairs is the opportunity for a full-tuition ride. One is for one of my peers. The second is for one of the parents. Theirs can be used for them, a child or a friend. Third, I am endowing a $50,000 scholarship to the Adult Education program I am graduating from for them to use as they see fit." Nicole turned and nodded to her professors with a smile. Their smiles were all she needed.

Nicole watched the people stand up and

look at the bottom of their chairs. Shouts of congratulations echoed in the large room.

As Nicole put the mic back at the podium, she congratulated the winners and stated, "I believe in all of you. Make your best life!"

With one more round of applause, the commencement continued. The figure in the back looked at Nicole with hatred. Her time was coming!

Nicole spent the rest of the time before receiving her diploma, thinking of all the work she'd put in. Negotiating her homework deadlines to consult with industry professionals to build her business for class credit. Working with local business help services such as Service Corps of Retired Executives and networking, she got enthusiastic buy-in to start her own business and get direction on how to build it.

Now, she was the proud owner of Learning Tide, which serviced the adult and K-12 industries. Nicole firmly believed that distance education could be adapted for most learning types. As she was fond of saying, anything was possible with time and money.

The sticking point came when organizations put off learning until it was needed immediately. By teaching organizations to be prepared and move with changing business needs, they could avoid the dreaded "fast-good-cheap" model. You can have two of the three, but you can't have all three. Well, under Nicole's business model, you could have all three. All it took was planning. And the pandemic helped.

When COVID-19 hit, everyone was looking for the impossible. Using a few local schools as test cases, Nicole was able to build her K-12 business quickly. With her assembly-line approach and use of unemployed K-12 teachers, she produced engaging e-learning programs that met all learning types' needs.

The same applied to her adult education side, which encompassed training for front-line workers. It took some sleepless nights and some chances on recruiters and staff of contractors, but it was well worth it.

As a result, business exploded. It came faster than Nicole expected, and it came at more than a monetary benefit to her. Nicole was able to create a portfolio that allowed her credit for her classes, and she was able to further her company.

Learning Tide boasted a core staff of 150 and a large consultancy group in all 50 states. Her next goal was to open European satellite offices in Ireland and one in Germany. Being centrally located, she could more easily oversee her operations, reach customers, and take some fabulous trips. A separate foundation was about to start significant fundraising to provide public education and other training to countries that wanted and needed it.

But it didn't stop there. Nicole had a successful line of books for people who wanted to learn about e-learning theory and practical application. These books were sold worldwide and used in classes her consultants taught to clients. While creating e-learning from self-paced to engaging live e-learning was great, Nicole also wanted to empower organizations to do things independently.

She was indeed on her way, and she allowed herself a cosmic sigh of relief.

TWELVE

The wind whipped her long red hair around her face. It flew like a blazing fire behind her as she sped toward home. Nicole was almost to the turnoff that was three miles away from her home. She was happy to be back and glad to get on with the rest of her working vacation. Nicole instructed the office not to call her. She had complete trust that they could handle whatever came up over the next two weeks.

Suddenly, a long, loud beep interrupted her thoughts. A big, classic Chevy truck painted robin's egg blue pulled up next to her. A furry-faced little man with tobacco-stained smiling teeth spoke.

Shaking her head as if she couldn't hear him, he yelled, "Wanna go out on a date?"

Nicole shook her head, frowning.

He was persistent. He leaned farther out and said, "Come on, babe, be a sport. Pull over. Let's talk about it." His thinning brown hair was wind greasy and stuck to the side of his head.

Nicole shook her head again and looked at the road ahead. She could see a car coming in the opposite direction. *Let's see him play chicken.* Smiling, she slowed down a bit—almost to the actual speed limit.

The bedraggled man leered at her and said, "That's good. I knew you wanted to talk to me. My name is Jimmy. Let's get off the road."

Nicole could see the driver of the truck pulling on Jimmy's arm. Inwardly, Nicole thought, he must have seen the oncoming car.

"I don't know if I can trust you." Nicole shouted, batting her eyes.

"All I want to do is talk with you. That's all." Jimmy licked his cracked split lips, brown spittle dribbling down his bearded chin.

What tripe, she thought, stifling an urge to roll her eyes and vomit at the same time. *What you want is to screw me, maybe let your friend have a go, leave me, and steal the bike.* Nicole smiled wolfishly, "That's all? Really?"

"Yes, now pull over!" Jimmy was becoming impatient. He turned to his friend. "What?" The driver said something to him, and Jimmy looked ahead. The car was about a mile away and coming fast.

Jimmy whirled back to her, "Move over." His friend started to ease the truck over.

Nicole eased closer to the truck. "Let's

play a game of chicken. The last one to swerve gets what they want." she challenged him.

Jimmy smiled a superior grin and licked his lips again, "You got it. Get ready to pay."

Nicole could see the car coming towards the truck and looked in her own mirrors. *No one in the back? Very good. No one in front? Way fucking good.* She eased over closer to the middle of the road, and the truck eased closer to her as well. This way, it gave them both an equal place in front of the oncoming traffic.

Both the bike and the truck sped forward, racing neck to neck. Jimmy's fat lips were wet with spit and pieces of chewing tobacco, and now and then, he looked at her and licked them. Just a little more. The oncoming car came closer and closer, and when Nicole could see the passengers in the car, she swerved back into her lane.

Nicole watched the other car sheer away from Jimmy and his friend. She turned her head as their truck came to a rocking stop in the drainage ditch. Slowing down, she spun the bike hard and looked back at the pair. The car was safely gone after ragging on Jimmy and his buddy, but the Chevy hadn't fared so well. Even from her view, she could see Jimmy get out of the cab and start yelling.

Laughing at his predicament, Nicole raised her arms in victory. OK, she had swerved first, but she still had a vehicle that worked, and she had gotten what she wanted.

Jimmy's screams of rage reached her ears, promising retribution. Nicole opened her jacket and lifted her t-shirt, flashing greasy Jimmy a fairy tale peek at her well-rounded berry-tipped breasts.

Jimmy stopped yelling momentarily, his jaw flapping open.

Pulling her t-shirt back down, Nicole shook her head and flipped the bird at him. *Fuck him. That will teach him to go around and try to pick up girls on the highway.* Then she turned and sped away. *Let him try to find me, the pervert.*

THIRTEEN

The modified bungalow was as she always remembered it. Once a schoolhouse later turned into a home, it was not grand but certainly big by normal standards. The white siding had been freshly painted that summer and still retained the new brightness against the brown and green trees surrounding it. The porch was simple with a waist-high brick wall and unadorned square wooden posts at the corners and either side of the concrete stairs that came down to greet visitors. The porch still looked comforting with the ever-present hanging porch swing and oversized chair next to it.

Home.

As her bike came to a stop, Nicole suddenly felt tired and glad to be there. This house was where her soul was, where she needed to be. Nicole slung her black leather saddlebags over her shoulder and carried her helmet. She could see the window to the sitting room was open a bit, and she could hear the TV playing.

She opened the unlocked front door, and she sat her things in the foyer.

Her mother came out of the kitchen. "So, you're back." She looked at Nicole with cold eyes. "What are you here for?"

"Relax, I won't disturb you." Nicole ascended the stairs to her room.

"Don't expect me to be around much." her mother called after her.

"I won't."

Nicole shook her head and walked to the kitchen, and looked around. Mrs. Tenant came in once a week to clean, and she would market for her as well. Today was no exception. The house was neat as a pin, and the fridge and pantry were stocked. A note from Mrs. Tenant indicated she would call the following week to discuss cleaning and pantry needs for the business headquarters.

However, today, something was amiss.

"Mrs. Tenant?" she called.

No answer.

The television was on. Nicole could understand if Mrs. Tenant was there and the tv was on. Mrs. Tenant loved her talk shows. If Mrs. Tenant was no longer in the house, she would have either turned off the television, or it would have automatically shut off after 30 minutes.

Nicole looked at the furniture. Dust-free. She felt the food in the fridge. Cold.

Weird. Perhaps Nicole's mother's ghost was being lazy in death as in life.

She sat down to soak in her surroundings. Although she had only been gone a few days, she always loved coming back to the house. Somehow, she sorted out the building in her mind versus the people who were still haunting it and everything that happened. Nicole closed her eyes and breathed deeply.

Across the coffee shop, she could see Lane smiling at her. She could see other people around him, and he asked Nicole something that she couldn't hear. He bent down and picked something up—her first manuscript.

"Is this yours?" He asked again, a southern divine southern drawl punctuating his words. His blue eyes sparkled.

"What? Yes. Thank you." Nicole held her hand out for the papers.

"Distance Education: A Practical Approach?" His sandy eyebrows shot up.

"Yes, I'm a digital media major. This is for a project."

"Another geek." He flashed her a smile, his deep dimples pulling her into their beauty.

Nicole smiled, relaxing, "None other. I really need to go." She took the manuscript and started to walk away, wishing she had more time to talk with this gorgeous man. She couldn't stop thinking of how his hazelnut brown hair framed his face like a halo.

"Maybe we will meet again, Nicole Bichey."

So he noticed the name on her book. Smiling to herself, Nicole turned around and hoping she seemed calmer than she felt, "Maybe so."

As she turned to leave again, he asked, curiously, "Don't you want to know my name?"

Raising her eyebrows, Nicole retorted, "Only when I see you again." and she left a gaping Lane Kincaid behind her.

Nicole felt so warm. It felt as if she were surrounded by a blanket of warmth, and she snuggled deeper into it. It seemed to engulf her, tighter and tighter.

"Nicole... Nicole..."

Not wanting to release the warmth, she frowned. What was that? Where was it coming from?

"Nico-o-ole-e-e..."

She could feel the warmth leaving her. Moaning, Nicole said, "What?"

"It's time to get u-u-u-u-p-p…"

Damn the ghosts in the house. Especially her parents. And what a false sense of warmth from memories of Lane. He could be charming, but under that charm lay a bitter bottle of bilious man-baby.

She went into the kitchen and had a peanut butter and pickle sandwich and a small dish of strawberries. Afterward, she piled the dishes into the dishwasher. The house needed some updating, but she had installed a dishwasher post-haste after her parents' deaths. Nicole didn't even bother rinsing the dishes. "Econo washing" is what she liked to call it. Most people criticized her for her washing techniques. Well, not everyone, just Lane really, but she just couldn't be bothered with cleaning. It was a necessary evil she hated. Why rinse the dishes if they were going in a dishwasher? Anything to finish quickly.

Even as eager as she was to be done with her chores, Nicole allowed her mind to wander as she looked out the kitchen window at the darkening sky. The smell of dirt and dried corn stalks wafted to her through the partially opened window. There was absolutely nothing better than Fall.

The house had many ghosts, and Nicole lived with them as she would another person. She had not cleansed the home of any of the spirits. Besides her parents, the house had at least two men, a teenage boy, and two women. She and Renee had made their acquaintances by accident over the years they lived in the home. Nicole was unsure of all of their origins, but she sensed quite a bit.

A few specters were pissed at something that happened in their lives, and some seemed sad. Most rarely made a physical appearance but created more noise than anything. Her parents were just annoying, and she annoyed them right back by not doing what they asked or indicated. Mom liked to wake her up, and she slept in to piss her off. Not that she'd been able to do that in a while. She also liked to keep her room somewhat messy as a teen, and although she'd gotten better as an adult, out of necessity if nothing else, she still left it enough of a mess to piss off her mother.

Her dad rarely made an appearance, much like real life. When her mother got pissed as a spirit, she could feel her dad trolling. Only occasionally did she say she'd send them back where they belonged. The threat usually kept them at bay for a while. Now that Nicole was established and had time to breathe, she would have to do something about the leftover guests.

It was like that with Lane, too. She had to keep him at bay in one way or another. Lane couldn't be bothered with things like nature, that he never realized how beautiful it could be. He didn't seem to exhibit any more profound emotion than where to party or what was the quickest way to get off.

Worst of all, his idea of fun was a movie and a romp through the nearest bar. "Just one beer," he would say. "Just one beer" would turn into two and four and then all-nighters—something Nicole couldn't stomach. She had goals that didn't include going on weekly or nightly benders. Towards the end of their relationship, when she had pointed this out to him, his reply had been, "I have quicker ways to make money."

Nicole was mystified by his comment and asked for an explanation. He smiled and told her that his parents may pay for his tuition at the nearby Indiana State University, but his tight allowance wouldn't cover everything else. He showed her the little dresser put inside his closet for the sake of space, and there she was, half shocked to find a stash of marijuana and pills.

Not that marijuana was harmful, Nicole considered it no worse than alcohol, but it was the pills and illegal part that had stunned her. True, he could make good money from students willing to pay for a bit of joy, but to jeopardize everything he had been working for? Nicole tried this reasoning with him, but all he did was shrug and say, "That's what my parents are for."

The drugs and attitude should have been her warning then that things just weren't right with Lane. But if anything, his drinking should have tipped her off. His drinking was ultimately out of control. If he wasn't in class or studying, he was always in the process of coming off of or creating a hangover. Ok, sometimes getting drunk wasn't a bad thing. Every weekend, every weeknight that proceeded a no class weekday, and all holidays were more than a bit excessive. It was to the point that she didn't want to go anywhere with him.

And then that made things worse.

Towards the end of their relationship, if they couldn't go out or get drunk, Lane would move on to the final plan for most of his evenings— sex.   Nicole had to admit, sex wasn't really good with Lane, sober or drunk. He certainly wasn't like Michael Madigan had been. She found the longer they were together, the feelings she thought they had felt in the beginning were somewhere in the distance, and Nicole felt like she was just a hole for him. Never again, resolved Nicole, placing the last knife in the dishwasher.

She bent to shut the door, and the knife popped out and spun by its handle on the floor. I must have jiggled it loose when I moved the door, she thought. Picking it back up, she carefully moved it to the top rack.

FOURTEEN

The kitchen was a large warm room. It was a typical farmer's style kitchen that was open and airy. It was connected to the family room, where, in earlier days, her parents couch planted, watching tons of television. Mom watched predominantly Catholic programs, and both parents watched news and wholesome sitcoms. Her dad chain-smoked, and her mom binge ate.

Family gatherings intensified the smoke and food. Not that the family gatherings were all that. Mostly with her dad's family, it ended in an argument, and with her mother's side, it ended in silence as it was now.

Nicole heated the tea kettle.

When her parents, Lindsey and Dee Bichey, died five years ago. Nicole's aunts and uncles had the nerve to swoop in, sniffing for a handout. They left far more swiftly and with an acrid taste in their mouths when they were given nothing. After that time, the other remaining family, with whom they were not particularly close, seemed to scatter to the earth's four corners.

Despite the death of her parents, the house was Nicole's solace. Over the years, she lived in the home, and when she returned from extended times at school, she realized it was a retreat now, no matter its past. She had always loved living in the country and the house. When the cool breezes blew through the home and the night critter cacophony began, she was utterly content.

The cool fall evenings and the warm spring mornings seemed to rejuvenate her. Instead of oppression, she saw the house as a home and her primary place of business. And she was thankful she could use it as her refuge.

She sat at the big oak trestle table and looked at her parent's chairs. Every Sunday, it was always the same with her sister, Renee.

"Lindsey, Renee didn't talk in church again today!" Dee snapped.

"I'm not sure what you want me to do about it," her father sardonically replied.

"Talk to her! She needs to respond in church!"

Lindsey put down his Salem Premium Long, letting it burn in the amber glass ashtray supported by a horse post. Sighing, he trudged resolutely and measuredly to Renee's room.

That's when the screaming began. And the spanking.

"See, you pissed yourself, didn't you? Clean that up! And next time, do what your mother says!"

But that wasn't even the worst memory she had to reconcile. The last time she saw her parents or her sister was the memories she had to face. A therapist had been beneficial in that respect.

Nicole sighed and poured tea. Although she wished her parents would have cared enough to want to know about her life or even to want to know her, she knew that was far from the truth. Her parents cared for no one but themselves.

Not even each other. Lindsey Bichey had been tall, dark-haired, dark-eyed, and swarthy-skinned from his Native American heritage. He was a brilliant man who was as debilitatingly cold and unfeeling as his wife.

Dee Bichey was a bitter woman. Cold brown eyes and equally flat brown hair cut in an unflattering old lady was and set made Dee look much older than she ever was. Although her hair became threaded with gray over the years, Nicole thought it had matched her icy and detached nature. Dee was as unconcerned for her family as she was for her husband. Nicole knew Dee never wanted children. She read it in her mother's diary when she was 12 years old.

Too often, Lindsey and Dee remained in fathomless silence. Lindsey with his demons and Dee with her god. Because they couldn't control themselves, they tried to control her whole life down to who she dated. They didn't want her to talk or become independent. Nicole concluded that they saw the girls as extensions of their missed opportunities. That just made Nicole and her sister strive more for independence.

Her sister. That was a completely different story. She felt a pang of conscience.

Nicole took a big drink of strong Irish tea. She drained the cup and went to the cupboard, and took the rum bottle down. Pouring a healthy glug into her teacup, Nicole stared into her cup, remembering the conversation she overheard.

"Now, Peony—"
"Don't you 'now Peony' me, Henry Rutledge. Those girls have lost their parents,

as poor examples as they were. What they need right now is a hot meal, warm sheets, and good sleep. I'll put them in the spare room. You can deal with what to do with them tomorrow."

Sheriff Rutledge knew better than to argue with his wife. Still, they had a killer on the loose. "Take them home and lock the door. I am going to be a while."

Nicole took another long swallow, and the liquid burned its way down her throat the way tears of relief flowed down her face that night. Although she was in shock that her parents were dead, she couldn't muster much sympathy.

Now, it was time to move forward and make this house her own. This was the beachhead on which Nicole would take complete control of her life.

FIFTEEN

That evening, Nicole went for another ride on her bike. Despite wanting to relax and get rid of the business pressure she felt, Nicole couldn't. Her mind was used to working more than a mile a minute. At 11:45 p.m., she slung her saddlebags on her bike. Riding down the wooded back roads of Grant County, Nicole let out a tremendous yell. It felt so good to let herself just go.

The trees were nothing more than dim outlines against the midnight blue sky. Her single headlight picked out beasties at the side of the road. Rabbits, possum, and other animals out scavenging before winter seemed to be ghostlike lumps with shining eyes in the tall dried summer weeds in the drainage ditch on either side of the road.

Nicole kicked her bike up another gear and took the hill before the old bridge at 80 miles per hour.

The bridge was one of the last handful of surviving wooden bridges that allowed vehicular traffic in Indiana. It's real name was Holiday Bridge, but everyone called it the

Screaming Bridge. Situated on a low traffic road, it was rumored that if you parked your car on the old bridge at midnight, you wouldn't be able to start your car again, and you would hear the gruesome wails of a child who had been killed on the bridge in a car accident. Some even said that the ghoulish white figure of a woman, searching for her child, would cross behind the car.

She came here with Renee one night. They hadn't seen the woman, but at midnight they had heard what sounded like the wail of a child.

The bridge was dark when she approached it. No one was there. Oh, what the hell, Nicole thought, why not? She pulled her bike up on the wide, dusty wooden planks and let her bike idle for a minute. Then she shut the motor off, leaving the headlight on. It was silent except for the crickets and an occasional stirring of dried leaves. Nothing to be afraid of. It's all an urban legend. Nicole checked her digital watch. 11:57 p.m. *Cool.*

With a quick movement, Nicole shut the light off to leave herself in complete darkness. She could no longer see the outline of trees even after her eyes adjusted to the darkness. The moon didn't penetrate the area of trees where the bridge was. She had always found that an interesting footnote to the whole story.

Nicole turned herself around on the bike to face how she had come and took off her brown bomber jacket. Come on, white lady, come and see me. A barn owl hooted in the distance. *Hoot-hoot to you, too,* she thought, lacing her fingers behind her head. She rested her heavy Caterpillar boots on the back of her bike's seat and started to hum. *I guess the child and mother have found each other.*

Closing her eyes, Nicole absorbed the night. No people, no work, just quiet. Due to her introverted nature, work was sometimes a jungle in Nicole's eyes. She breathed in the pungent night air— drying leaves and the promise of cooler weather. Nothing could be better.

A crack of a twig brought Nicole out of her thoughts. So the midnight lady is here. Nicole waited, peering into the darkness. Anytime now. Her heart was racing with excitement. When the woman didn't appear, Nicole called out, "You're late. You're going to lose your reputation if you don't hurry."

Nicole heard the shuffling of leaves and

the crack of more twigs. In the distance, she heard the crickets. Then nothing but the blood pounding in her ears.

If it wasn't the ghost woman, who was it? Maybe it was Jimmy from the Chevy. Nicole's smile split the dark. That little prick had more coming to him than he thought. If he was so fucking angry about his truck, wait till he tried to touch her. She'd give him a proper taste of what was meant by "I am woman hear me roar."

Nicole listened for a moment. From the darkness, she could hear a figure emerging from the trees to her right.

Not saying a word, she reclined against her bike. It wasn't the white woman, it seemed, after all. Waiting, Nicole stared into the pitch-black night.

SIXTEEN

Nothing, human or not, was coming. She hadn't heard anything for a couple minutes. The white lady and the child were obviously on holiday or together at last. Whatever she heard was seemingly uninterested in her. Nicole was disappointed. It would have made for a good story.

Sighing, Nicole dropped her feet noisily to the rough planks and mounted her bike once more. Nicole wasn't tired and had extra energy. Perhaps it was some sort of adrenaline letdown from the hard work she had put in. At any rate, Nicole didn't want to go home and watch TV. She didn't want to go to bed. Everything was closed, and, for the third time this evening, she lamented the fact she was let down by the spiritual.

Nicole had to speak with the general contractor about the home remodel in the morning. She supposed she should go home to be at her best that conversation.

But she couldn't make herself go. The night was still warm. It was strange weather for that time of year, even for Indian Summer.

Some said it was all from an El Nino, and some said it was because the end of the world was coming. Nicole personally thought it was global warming.

Nicole decided to go for a swim. It would burn off some energy and make her sleepy. Maybe she would take away the ache between her legs while she was there. She started her bike and maneuvered it off of the bridge and into the woods to her left. This was where she began to learn hope, to dream, and to love. The recent onslaught of men certainly had woken something up in her.

She parked her bike and dug for a towel from her bags. Nicole was always prepared, like in *Hitchhiker's Guide to the Galaxy*. Picking her way through the half overgrown path with the aid of her keychain flashlight, she finally came to the edge of the pond. The giant oak tree stood with its branches cradling the pond.

The leaves were beginning to fall, and their dry tartness tickled her nose. The waters were still, and the air was thick with insects singing their nightly lullaby. She tossed her towel onto an old tree stump and sat down to remove her boots and jacket. She threw her shirt and jeans on the ground.

Dressed in only her lacy black bra and matching panties, she plunged into the water. It felt delicious on her skin.

"Twice in one day after almost four years. How fortunate I am," Nicole heard a familiar voice say.

Swinging around, Nicole gasped. With the moonlight as a backdrop, she could see a prominent figure approaching her. Michael Madigan. As soon as he stepped into view, she recognized his tousled hair and hooded eyes that she knew to be an incredible shade of gray ringed by a darker gray. The memory of their time here came flooding back.

Her eyes narrowed. "You!" she exclaimed. "What are you doing here?"

"I live here. Remember?" The smile Nicole remembered played about his sensual full lips.

"You live here? You?" She repeated dumbly.

"Yes, all my life. My mother died two years ago. I inherited this." He sat down on the ground near her clothing, his intense eyes looking into hers. He offered Nicole her T-shirt, never losing eye contact.

"I'm sorry. I was so busy with school..." She stepped out of the water, took the shirt, and slipped it over her head. "What are you doing here so late?" She knew it sounded dumb.

"I know. I appreciated the flowers and card you sent." He shrugged, not seeming to notice. "I just finished training and have a break. I was restless, and I know that the kids still come out here sometimes and look for the White Lady. I heard the bike." He shrugged and smiled. "It's been a while, Nicole."

"Yes, it has." Nicole was trying to absorb everything. She struggled to get her still wet legs to cooperate in the jeans' leg holes and experienced dejá vu. Nicole felt as if Michael were owed an explanation, but she couldn't get her mouth and mind to cooperate. Nicole noticed that he continued to look elsewhere as she dressed. Ever the gentleman despite their history.

Tossing her red hair back and securing it with a long leather band, she looked at Michael, "I thought cops kept to a regular bedtime."

"I'm not a cop exactly. I am a cop who is a detective in training," he grinned, revealing his even white teeth.

"That means you should still be in bed." Her voice was tinged with sarcasm.

"Still fresh as ever, I see." He slyly looked

at her, "You've certainly done well. Graduating, creating an empire." He crossed his legs and laid down, looking at the sky.

Nicole's eyes narrowed defensively, "How do you know so much about me?"

"What can I say? Mr. Swayne is a fountain of information. And your name is all over the Internet."

Nicole started to pull on her boots. She shivered. The night air must be getting colder, or so she told herself.

"What's your hurry? Earlier, you didn't look like you were going to be leaving soon."

She raised an eyebrow, "That's because I was alone. Now that you are here, I think I should be going before you try to charge me for using the pond again."

"I think you liked the kiss. Besides, I gave you your towel first, didn't I? And today I gave you your T-shirt. Tell me, do you make a practice of being enchantingly naked in the moonlight?"

Nicole put her things in her saddlebags and got onto her bike. "I think your memory is faulty. I wasn't naked then or now. Goodbye."

"You weren't saying goodbye to me at the Pump and Go."

Nicole started her bike and steered away from the pond. She felt odd that they had never resolved things, and she was in no mood to deal with it tonight. And she couldn't think of a thing to say to him.

"Wait, don't go. I want to talk to you."

"I don't think we have anything to talk about." Nicole was thankful her bike drowned out his laughter.

Sleep did not come easily. As she lay in bed, Nicole wondered what would have happened had she stayed.

SEVENTEEN

The following day, Nicole was awake with the sun, her eyes feeling the warmth of the sun on them. Indian Summer is still here, she thought. No time to be lazy. Stretching her shapely sun-browned legs, Nicole wiggled her toes and could feel herself tingling.

Flinging her blankets back, she let the sun stream over her naked body. Nicole couldn't stand to wear pajamas. They made her too warm. Her nipples tightened as Nicole ran her fingers over them, feeling the warm, smooth skin under her fingers. Pressing her legs together to stifle the ache between them, Nicole ran her hands across her breasts and her belly. She tickled her belly button with her fingers, stroking lightly. Mmm.

She looked over at the mirror on her dresser. What she saw in it beckoned her hand downward, and she opened the silky folds of flesh. From her vantage point, she could see herself glistening, and she ran her fingers over the sticky wetness. Nicole shivered slightly, making her swollen nipples jiggle.

She closed her eyes. Lane. It had been

a long time since she had been with him, but Nicole could still remember the first time with him.

He took her to a movie and then back to his apartment, paid by Mommy and Daddy's allowance. It was on his narrow bed Lane had taken her; the sensation of having someone other than Michael inside her was intoxicating. Lane had rasped all sorts of endearments to her—how much he loved her and always would. She snorted. Endearments were nothing to him.

As she worked her fingers frantically, Nicole suddenly remembered how the quality analyst filled her. It almost put Lane's to shame. And Michael...She remembered what Michael had been like that energetic and enlightening afternoon by the pond. Despite his lack of experience, Michael was still the gold standard.

The first waves came quickly, making her head pound with the sensation. She moaned loudly and collapsed on the bed, pressing her legs together to relieve her sweet after ache.

It had been so long! Too much time spent on work, Nicole grimly thought. The quality analyst had awakened her sexual feelings again. And for that, she wished him well. An after-shock of pleasure shuddered through her.

Her head dangled over the side of the bed as she thought about her day. Working with the contractors and then a day of wandering was just the thing. Nicole longed for the outdoors. But work came first.

Reluctantly, she arose, feeling her juices sliding down her legs. She reached between her legs, and another thrill raced through her. Raising her sticky hand to her lips, she licked her fingers, enjoying the taste of herself. Heaven.

The figure watching Nicole snarled.

Nicole called out, startled. "Hello?" That would not have been her parents; they never snarled but only hurled insults and popped up at bad times. Nicole wondered which it was.

She heard a car door slam. Peeking out her window, she saw the contractor tilt his hat way back on his head. He was noisy and far too early. Nicole sighed. Better get this over with.

"This house is taking major renovations to get it to where you want it. Why not just tear it down and start again?"

"Because," Nicole stated more patiently to the contractor than she felt, "I wouldn't have a place to stay, and this house has sentimental value."

The general contractor, Dave Schipp, and his framer, Ted Waller, had been discussing plans for the last hour, and they seemed none too keen to take the project on.

"Didn't some people die here a few years ago?" Ted asked. "It seems there was a couple —"

"That couple was my parents," Nicole stated coldly. "Gentlemen, my engineers said you were highly skilled. If this project isn't something you want to take on, please let me know so I can engage someone else."

"Now hold on, we never said that!" Dave protested.

Nicole held up her hand, "No, but you've tried to dissuade me at every turn. What I am asking for is very simple. Repair the plaster. Paint. Mill trim work. Add two bathrooms, create a breezeway to the new business center." She looked at them harshly, "What it boils down to is some excavation, masonry, framing, drywall, roofing, electrical, and plumbing. Can your organization handle leading the project or not? I assume when you were chosen for the project, you were familiar with it."

A car approached, and Nicole excused herself, leaving the two gobstruck men in her wake. *What now?* Nicole looked at the car's occupant. Michael.

"Yes?" Nicole asked as the car rolled to a stop.

"I heard you're looking for some contracting work."

"So? You're a cop." Nicole clipped the last word.

"Nicole, please. I am here to help. I don't want you to be taken advantage of."

Nicole snorted.

"I have experience with construction. I worked as a laborer in high school in the summer. I just thought you might need help. You can't be great at everything. Nobody is that perfect." Michael smiled a little crookedly.

"Well... they are fractious despite my vetting process."

"Great," Michael smiled, and Nicole's world lit up. "Let's go."

It rankled her that the men responded to Michael better than with her. With Michael's help, Nicole was finally able to get the contractor to agree to her terms.

The original house would have minimal changes to it. Nicole already had the plaster and woodwork restored two years ago. The walls had been painted a year ago. The significant concessions would be the attic which would become her private office, a new back stairway from the kitchen to that the office with a deck, and the current kitchen would be combined with the original schoolroom to create an open plan.

Nicole's bedroom and other bedrooms would be updated with a shared bathroom between the guest rooms and a private one for her room. A secret door would lead between the two bathrooms to give her access to the house's front but keep her office private.

The rest of the downstairs rooms would be changed slightly as well. Nicole's parents' room would become part of the living room. The laundry room would be relocated to the basement, and the old laundry room marked a part of the business area and would be expanded to become an outdoor deck.

A whole new building mirroring her house from the outside would be added with a large conference room, room for a personal assistant to work on-site if necessary, a party room for entertaining and educating, and upper and lower balconies.

Finally, the garage and barn would be remodeled, and a covered walkway between the buildings would be added. When people walked from building to building, they wouldn't have to walk through mud or get wet.

The electrical, plumbing, and HVAC would be upgraded to accommodate the additional need. Next year, the outside would be relandscaped so that the front retained its charm and the back opened into a lush wildflower and native plant gardens and paths. Nicole hoped to make the space an Indiana meets Japanese garden. This fall, trees would be planted to give the acreage a wooded look. The covered walkways would be built to fit into this landscape.

Of course, the general contractor needed to work up the final numbers, but her engineers felt confident the campus could be achieved for 2.5 million dollars. Nicole smiled at the figure. It was a great deal of money. Due to her knack for working with people and the staff who worked with her, she had amassed ten times that amount in her personal finances. Her company was flush and debt-free.

Her grand plan was to create an estate-like feel to her property. After she and Michael spoke to the contractor, he kept her company while Nicole baked a cake for the Gutzwillers. She made a smaller cake for them to share. By the end of the conversation, they agreed to meet for dinner later in the week.

Then Nicole walked to her neighbors, the Gutzwillers, with a freshly baked cranberry Christmas cake, a decadent concoction of brown sugar, flour, butter, and eggs whipped with a ton of tart, fresh cranberries. The resulting cake had a crisp, thin sugar crust and moist cake that melted in one's mouth.

Nicole had a particular reason for visiting. First, they had been so kind to her as a child and after her parents died. Not once had they ever asked for anything from her, even after she came into money. Despite telling them she could provide for Renee, they still insisted on sending her a little money and a letter every month. They were better people than she was. She was so busy that she sent Renee money but sent letters sporadically.

Second, now that they were getting on in years, she wanted to help them as they had helped her. They lived in a small mid-century ranch home that they had built themselves. Recently, the Gutzwillers put their home and farm on the market. They used to have over 160 acres but sold it off in 20-acre parcels over the years. Now, they had 40 acres left, and she wanted to buy it and the house. Her attorney, Mr. Jacobs, spoke to them a few weeks earlier about her offer.

The cake was to truly sweeten the deal. "Mr. and Mrs. Gutzwiller, the way your house is situated so close to mine, literally across the road, would make an excellent guest cottage for visiting employees and friends. Your barn could easily be preserved and transformed into event space and rented out for special occasions."

The Gutzwillers were overjoyed. Instead of their home being torn down, it would still serve as a happy place. The barn would stay. And best of all, they wouldn't have to pay a commission to a real estate agent.

"I know Mr. Jacobs spoke with you about the timeline. And I want to make sure you're comfortable with it. As he mentioned, I have contractors coming to do floors and painting in my home and would like them to do the same in yours to save money. I have some employees staying close to Christmas and want to give them a homier feel versus a hotel. If they have to travel during the holidays, I want them to do it in comfort. I would have them stay with me, but my house is going to be a construction site due to upgrades and not very comfortable—even for me."

The pair looked at each other. Since the attorney visited, they had already started packing. Her price was fair. She offered their asking price plus 10% more in moving expenses. Since they were doing the packing and weren't moving very far away, they were still money ahead. And she had always been such a sweet girl, cursed with bad parents. And poor Renee, she sat in jail. While they couldn't condone what she had done, they could certainly understand why. The Gutzwillers nodded their agreement.

"Excellent! Mr. Jacobs will bring the papers by today if that is OK. Once you've had your attorney review them and they are signed, I can have a cashier's check to you for $170,000 within 24 hours."

EIGHTEEN

Now, what did she want?

Peeking through the curtains, Nicole couldn't believe she saw Lena arrive. Lena never did anything in a small way. Her naturally dark legs looked perfect with a pair of bright blue shorts and a white shirt. Lena stepped out of the car and said something to the driver.

What the hell? Jeremy Charrier?

Showing her perfect white teeth, Lena smiled at the person and waved as they drove on. She hoisted her backpack and suitcase.

Oh, goody-goody. She thinks she is staying.

Lena turned and looked at Nicole. *Just smile.* She ran up the stairs to the porch, where Nicole stood at the door.

"Nicole!" Lena yelled, pulling off her black Ray-Bans. Her chocolate eyes sparkled with excitement.

"Hey," Nicole said vaguely, not really conveying mutual excitement.

"Car is in the shop. Since I was bumming a ride and Jeremy needed to get back to Indy, we didn't even stop for lunch." Her long wavy black hair was pulled into a messy bun. Strands of hair framed her face. Lena brushed them absently back.

"So, what's up with you and Jeremy?" Nicole asked casually, leaning against the door frame, her arms crossed.

Lena rolled her eyes, "Absolutely nothing! He's only a friend." Seeing Nicole's disbelieving look, Lena added, "He already has a girlfriend."

"And when has that ever been a problem?" Nicole stated. "You can always find a way around that."

"Not this time," Lena said absently, and Nicole let the subject drop.

"What are you doing here?" Nicole asked through the screen door, not even inviting her in.

Lena sobered quickly. *Keep it together*, she told herself. "I need to talk to you. About Lane. And some other stuff."

"Lane? I haven't even talked to you or seen you since our encounter on campus."

"I know, and I am sorry about that. I was out of line." Lena sounded contrite.

Well, this is a change, Nicole thought skeptically.

"Nicole, I really need to talk to you. I

know things went south with us in school. And I am sorry. Please, just listen." Lena pleaded in desperation.

"You hungry?" Nicole sighed, "I am." Nicole didn't believe her. And Lena was nuts if she thought she was staying.

They went to the kitchen, and Nicole looked in to see what she had. "We have smoked sausage and mashed potatoes, or we can have soup. I bought some corn on the cob and tomatoes yesterday. I have some eggs, bacon..."

"The sausage, mashed potatoes, corn, and tomatoes. Breakfast food is overrated."

Nicole put the sausage in the skillet and microwaved the potatoes. Then, she and Lena shucked some corn and threw it in a pot of water. "The last of the season," Nicole said. Finally, Lena sliced some red and yellow tomatoes and put them on a plate to share. As they waited for the sausage, corn, and potatoes, they ate the sun-ripened tomatoes.

"So, what did you want to talk about?" Nicole asked Lena as they sat down, "What's this about, Lane?"

Lena hesitated, "It was all over the newspaper this morning."

"Really? What?" Nicole said distractedly as she took a bite of tomato. "I've been busy with contractors."

Lena shifted in her seat, "Seems Lane got busted for drugs."

Nicole stopped mid-bite. "What?" she said incredulously. "How did that happen?"

"It seems the police had been trying to crack a campus drug ring, and someone tipped them off about him. 'An unidentified source,' the newspaper said." She laughed, "At first, I thought it was you. But then I knew you wouldn't do that to Lane. I know you were upset when you broke up, but you wouldn't destroy his career because of it. And besides, it's been so long..."

Nicole digested this as she chewed her corn. She looked the news up on her phone. Sure enough, Lane's mug shot was plastered over the pages of the Internet. This news was much more delicious than she expected. "Destroy his career? What is all that? His parents have cash. He'll get out of it."

"Not that easy. It seems the police suspect Lane of being a leader, and the cops don't want to let him out on bail. They busted him late last night. Apparently, he was still half-drunk when they busted him.

Nicole thought about how close she could have been to that hot mess, and she was glad she made the right choice now for more than one reason. Nicole protested, "I knew he dealt marijuana and some pills, but I never saw him sell more than a couple joints to weekend partiers!" Nicole shook her head.

"The police found pot, meth, and Special K. He also had dipper drugs for the hard joints he sold. His apartment and car were full of it." Lena said quietly.

Nicole looked at her unbelievingly. "I can't believe it."

"They have enough to put him away for quite a few years. Supposedly, the informant gave them a taped statement and a signed statement in exchange for anonymity. The person mentioned days, times, and other dealers he sold to. They already said they are not interested in plea-bargaining to get him off. The newspaper reported that the DEA—yes, this is that serious— 'he will do hard time.' I guess the statement and what they found must be pretty good if they say that. I can show you the link later."

"OK, so he had some drugs. Does that

make him a drug czar?"

Lena shrugged, "Maybe, maybe not. The fact is, even with all his parents' influence, they won't be able to get him off. Not this time. He's in for the long haul." She saw Nicole's expression and felt a bit contrite. "I'm sorry about this."

It was Nicole's turn to shrug. "Why are you sorry? I saw the pot and pills. I told him he needed to be careful. His parents only ever threw money at him. If what the newspaper says is true, this will screw his career options."

Lena nodded and lapsed into silence.

Nicole studied her former friend. It seemed like there was something Lena wasn't telling her. "Spill it."

"What?"

"Lena, you and I have known each other too long for this. What's up?"

Lena's pitch-black brows drew together in a debate. "I didn't want to throw all of this on you at once."

"Lena, for god's sake, what is all this concern for me. After you unfriended me after our sleepover, I find this so hard to believe."

Lena looked down at the table. "I was the one he called when- when it happened. I immediately called his parents. They flew up early this morning from Tennessee, and we went to see him today. He looked awful."

Nicole leaned back in her chair and grasped the tall oak back. "So? Lane and I haven't exactly been on speed dial."

Lena continued to look at the table, refusing to meet Nicole's eyes. "As soon as his parents got there, he told them and me to leave. His parents looked like they could murder him. I got his parents out of the room and spoke to him. I couldn't tell what he was more concerned about- the drug charges or the fact that he laid down to go to sleep when he got home last night, and he said Renee visited him. She told him he was going to die by hanging."

Seeing Nicole's disbelieving look, she held up her hand, "I know, I couldn't believe it either. He was inconsolable. I finally gave him a hug and left the room. I spoke with his father before I left and told him to let me know if we could do anything." Lena finally looked up, "It was OK, wasn't it?"

Nicole shook her head. "I don't know what I can do for him. If it goes beyond his parent's ability and influence, then it surely goes beyond mine. Besides, I can't get involved. I have too many business plans coming up, and this would not look good. I have no doubt he is guilty of some drug activity. Did you tell his parents any of the conversations?"

Lena shook her head, "How could I tell them something like that?" She paused, "Maybe I should have. Then he would be considered crazy, maybe, and taken out of the general population."

Neither of them said anything for a while as they finished eating. "Lane must have been on something pretty bad to come up with that nonsense." Nicole mused out loud, "He will probably get beat up unless his parents can get him out of the general population."

"Nicole! How could you say something like that?" Lena barked sharply.

Nicole looked at Lena, "Well, it's true" She made shapes with her potatoes. She shook her head again, "Nope, I am sorry he made the choices he did, but I have a business reputation to protect."

"So what else did you want to talk about. You said you wanted to talk about Lane and stuff. What 'stuff'?"

Lena spoke slowly, "It's going to sound crazy."

"Just tell me what you want. Please. I don't have time for this."

Lena pressed her vaporizer button rapidly and took a deep drag. "This is what I wanted to talk to you about. Your sister is out, and she is going to kill me."

"This is outrageous. What is it with you and Lane and your fixation with Renee? Renee is still in the hospital. I can't get in, and she can't get out."

"But she is," Lena insisted, exhaling. A potent cherry aroma filled the room. "She was in my apartment last night after Jeremy left." She stumbled over the words.

"Oh, come now."

"She was!" Lena snapped, "She was, and she told me she was going to kill me."

"Don't you think that was just a dream? Perhaps you feel a little guilty for doing Renee's old boyfriend?"

Lena kept herself in check. She wanted to smack the smug attitude out of Nicole at the mention of her relationship with Jeremy. "No, it wasn't a dream. I should have never come here." Lena got up to leave.

"Oh, sit down. Was that it? A ghostly visit from my sister who is locked in a psychiatric hospital?"

"She told me Lane was going to die."

"He isn't going to be sentenced to death! He has multiple drug charges. He's going to do jail time."

"Nicole, Renee said he was going to hang."

"Even if he were to get the death penalty, which he won't because these charges aren't death penalty offenses, it would be lethal injection-"

Lena interrupted, "I know what I saw and heard. She is out there." Lena's cell phone rang. She took another puff on her cigarette and answered the phone, "Oh, shit," she murmured. "I am so sorry. Is there any-? No? Yes, I will look for it."

Lena hung up the phone. "Well, what do you think now? Lane is dead. They found him hanging by his shirt in his cell."

NINETEEN

After a silence that seemed to stretch on for hours after hearing of Lane's death, they decided they needed a distraction. "Let's get out of here." Nicole grabbed her keys. Soon the pair were speeding down the highway to Upland in her parents' Chevy Malibu. Not much to do there, but it did have the best ice cream store, Ivanhoe's.

They sat on the curb, Nicole eating a banana split and Lena a chocolate cookie sandwich. They ate in silence. It was warm for the late Summer, and Nicole was wearing denim shorts and a black lace tank top with her mass of red hair piled on top of her head. Strands curled around her face-framing it prettily. Lena was chic as ever with her flawless make-up.

"About Lane..." Lena began.

Nicole shrugged, "Not much to say."

"But the dream," Lena protested.

Holding up her hand, Nicole stopped Lena, "I don't know how to explain that. Maybe he said that to cover his suicide. Maybe he thought that would be easier for his parents."

They are in thoughtful quietness until Lena took notice of a young woman in the parking lot corner. The woman was chatting with a group and garnering much attention for her striking dark hair and tan and short white dress.

"I wonder if she's bi." Lena wondered aloud, taking in the young girl's rounded bottom, dark black hair, and honey gold skin.

Nicole gazed at Lena. She wasn't surprised Lena couldn't maintain any amount of deepness for longer than an hour.

"Oh come on, Nicole. Haven't you ever experimented a little?"

Nicole shook her head, "To each, their own."

A devilish gleam lit Lena's eyes, "It has nothing to do with taste. Just fun. And as I remember, you were always open to that. I would love to cover her little boobs in chocolate and lick it off."

"It would make them easier to find." Nicole commented dryly. "She seems a bit flat."

Lena giggled. "And I could find something between her legs." When Nicole didn't respond, Lena hinted, "Or it would be fun to get her on her knees and fuck her pussy while she licked me."

We could do that, the figure watching the pair thought. Mmmmm, how the figure would have loved to be the ice cream.

Lena felt a twinge between her legs. The idea suddenly appealed to her greatly. If Nicole had a business to protect, Lena could find a way to put it at risk. After all, in a way, Nicole owed her for everything unpleasant she'd had to do to get by. Besides, it could be fun; it had been a while since the spiritual guidance program. She owed Nicole for that.

After Nicole reported her to the Dean, the priest made her go to confession. The confessional was no longer the dark boxes with a wall between priest and penitent. It was an office with utilitarian furniture.

Once inside, Lena took a seat next to Father Branigan, who explained, "My child, the answer is so simple. We can give you guidance."

"Guidance how?"

He leaned forward, "We can't give you the spiritual guidance you need in a dorm. It would disturb the others. If you are off-campus, we could provide you with guidance without a bother.

"That sounds good, but I don't have the money..."

"But based on your behavior, someone would need to check in on you regularly. Keep you on the path of righteousness."

"How would this work?"

"You would have clerical and parental sponsors. In exchange for rent, you would be in a program with other girls where you would be required to confess regularly and meet at least three times a week with either clergy or parental sponsor. At least once a week confession until the clergy is satisfied with your progress."

"Three times a week and confession once a week?"

"At least three times a week. And confession as often as necessary." He put his hand on her knee, "The alternative is expulsion.'"

Lena knew she didn't have a choice. Her mother was dead, and her father was in hospice. She was at the school on a scholarship. She was two years away from getting her degree in liberal arts. Lena wanted out of her small town persona, and this was the way to get there. Besides, this wouldn't be the first time she got her kink on to get where she needed to be. It did sound potentially fun. Sure, Father

Branigan was old, but it was a new twist to add to her list of conquests. And she'd already been down the parental road. It might be hard to juggle Jeremy and her others, but it would be worth it to get off campus and plan revenge on Nicole.

"Ok, what do I need to do to get started?"

"I'll file weekly reports with the Dean. As long as all is satisfactory, nothing but your address changes." Father Branigan looked at her intently. "Shall we get started on your redemption?"

Lena nodded.

"Kneel and begin your confession." he instructed as he pulled his frock aside and unzipped his pants.

"Bless me, Father, for I have sinned..." she spoke between mouthfuls of his hairy cock.

From that time, the priest, other clergies, and an assortment of other visitors brought to the house patronized her off-campus house. True to their word, they scheduled their visits with her and the other girls. Sometimes they would show up two or three at a time, sometimes with a reticent novice in tow. The faces of the parent sponsors changed with regularity.

Lena had to give it to them. It was a well-organized operation. She couldn't prove it, but she suspected that the parents were making sizable donations for the privilege. The novices were obviously being scared into submission.

The girls she shared the house with were on birth control pills, but otherwise, it was a free-for-all in the bedroom. They were told that everyone had been medically vetted. The program didn't need that sort of trouble, they were told. But occasionally, when an infection did pop up, they had a plan for that. An old doctor would come by and give them what they needed. And later, at the follow-up, the girls repaid the favor.

Some of the others were in her situation where they had few options, but honestly, the girls were all horny and quite happy to fuck whoever was put in front of them. Especially when they got generous tips.

Graduation for the girls turned into a bacchanalia of unprecedented proportions. The house was turned into a revolving door of people. Priests and parents, and only they knew who else lined up in the place waiting outside doors, visiting multiple rooms until early graduation morning. Lena knew of more than one unwashed head of hair slicked into place under the graduation caps with their guests' leftover offerings.

Lena didn't mind the sex, but she hated being forced into the situation. Especially by Nicole. But it didn't matter anymore. Lena had her diploma, and she would have her revenge.

TWENTY

After Ivanhoe's, the women went to High Tunnel Tavern, a tribute to the town's early hope. Early settlers tried to get in on the canal project during the 1830s, but that didn't happen. Next came a run as a depot city on the Indiana Central Railroad.

The town's name came from the belief it was the highest point on the rail line from Columbus, Indiana, to Chicago, Illinois. Although it seemed to be more folklore than fact, tunnels were supposedly built by the railroad men when they put the railway through. In these tunnels, one of which was supposed to run under the establishment, all sorts of deprivation occurred. From opium to women, these tunnels had quite a reputation. Nicole had never seen the tunnels, and having lived here her whole life, she would have thought someone would have found them as Upland was not huge by any means.

The High Tunnel Tavern was a family restaurant by day, a sports bar in the afternoon, and a den of the devil at night, according to Taylor University, a Christian liberal arts college. The drinking and dancing made the bar strictly off-limits at any time of the day or night for students, faculty, and staff. If a student was found at the tavern or proven to have been on-premises, they were most certainly severely reprimanded, if not expelled.

For Nicole, the alcohol was cold, and the food was good, being known for fried pickles. The place was a little quiet for so early in the evening, and although sports shows were playing on the televisions, no sound could be heard. A foursome was setting up for live music.

The day had been exhausting, and Nicole was still trying to process what Lena said about Renee and the fact that Lane was dead. Nicole simply didn't know what to believe.

"I don't know about you, but that ice cream just made me more hungry." Lena commented, looking at the menu.

"I could go for some food." Nicole agreed.

They split fried pickles, and Lena got the ribeye. Nicole stayed with a habanero chicken salad. Both women had a Guinness and a tequila chaser.

Nicole let the alcohol course through her. It seemed much more rational when she was on her way to drunk. "Lena," Nicole began, "Did Lane's parents say anything other than what you told me?"

"No. But they sounded distraught."

"Of course they did. Their son was found hanged. Anyone with compassion would be upset." Nicole was surprised at how easy it was to say the words. She was sad, of course, but she did not feel the heart-wrenching gut tearing she would have if she still loved him. She felt vaguely sorry she didn't take more time to talk to him at the bar the other night, but he wasn't in the talking mood.

"I've been thinking about that business with your sister I told you about. I asked Jeremy-"

"Why would you ask Jeremy anything?"

"Jeremy is a leading occultist, you know, tarot cards and such. Apparently, he has quite the reputation. I asked him what he thought, and he said it was just a bad dream. He said there is no way she could be in two places at once."

Nicole didn't have time to process this or any other part of the days' revelations. She looked up and saw Michael Madigan roll in the door. Looking particularly good in his snug jeans and lightweight henley shirt, he moved gracefully through the crowd.

"I can't believe that is him." Lena breathed, licking her lips. "He never looked that good in high school."

"Put your pussy back in your pants," Nicole sweetly commented. Michael had seen the pair, and Nicole motioned for him to sit with them.

"What are you doing here?" He smiled at Nicole.

"Just grabbing some food, some drink. Lots of drink." Nicole smiled like the Cheshire cat.

"Apparently," he smiled. "Lena," he said shortly.

"Do you two remember each other?" Nicole brightly slurred.

Lena gave Michael her patented smile, guaranteed to wake up the drowsiest man, "I believe I remember you. You were a couple years older than us, right?"

"Try four." he smiled at her, then turned to Nicole, "Mind if I grab some food with you?"

"Not at all," Lena interjected.

Michael ordered a sirloin. While they waited for his food, they discussed everything from the weather, school memories, and what Lena was doing at school.

When his steak arrived, Michael ate like he was a ravenous animal.

"Don't you ever eat?" asked Nicole.

"Occasionally, but working out of town doesn't give me time to really cook."

Nicole was feeling relatively high from her beers and tequila. "When we have dinner, it should be at my house. I will cook for you."

Lena touched his arm, "Yes, we can cook for you."

The figure that had been watching them touched Lena's hand and concentrated. She yelped and removed her hand from Michael's arm.

"What is wrong with you?" Nicole asked Lena.

"Nothing."

Nicole gave her a sideways glance. She couldn't just leave Michael alone.

Michael seemed oblivious to Lena, much to her displeasure and much to Nicole's delight. "Do you want to dance, Nicole? Or are you steady enough on your feet?"

"Sure. Let's have a go."

The bar was more full than when the

women arrived, and the place smelled like alcohol, sweat, tropical perfume, and rich cologne. From her vantage point on the dance floor, Nicole could see tables full of half-eaten burgers, bits of ribs and chewed chicken bones, dabs of salads and their tangy dressings, and the remnants of half-melted ice in cups.

Judging from the looks on many of the people's faces at the bar, they were a ruin of broken dreams, bad days, and hell-bent revenge plans. At the beer garden just outside the building, the strategically placed shrubbery gave couples a chance to talk about sweet things away from the crowd and friends to enjoy their camaraderie without having to be heard over the music.

"What are you doing with her?" Michael asked incredulously.

"She showed up out of the blue." Nicole shrugged. She danced naturally to the thumping music. Her soft red hair, loosened from its clip, bounced gently around her shoulders and her green eyes were bright under the artificial light. She looked good in her cut-off jean shorts and clinging tank top, and in a completely unaffected way, Nicole knew it.

She smiled at the handsome young man

in front of her. Michael would certainly never win a fast dance contest, but he was trying and seeming to enjoy himself. It was of no consequence to Nicole as she was strangely happy just being with him in a way she never had been before. Nicole knew deep down that Michael was kind and intelligent, and she could see what fun he could be to be around. If Nicole didn't know better, she would almost say she was falling for Michael all over again.

Maybe she dated Lane trying to recreate what she had experienced with Michael. How wrong a girl could be!

In the ocean of dancers around them, jockeying to where she could get a better look at Michael, was Jo de Beauvoir. She was clearly the most breathtaking dancer, and she thought all those times she danced in her room to videos had paid off.

Jo wore a white eyelet linen mini tank dress showing off her small breasts and hard nipples to perfection, with matching white wedge shoes. Her dark hair was pulled back in a messy bun, and strands of curly hair spilled down her neck.

She was as local as they came, having grown up in Upland. Jo was dancing with another local, who she'd fucked a few times, but she wasn't really into him. While the local was trying hard to keep up with Jo's dance moves, she watched Michael.

That is what I want. Class and a sexy body all in one. A man with a job, so I don't have to work another day in my life.

She managed to dance her way over close and pointedly looked at Michael. She looked at him with her dark fringed brown eyes and rolled them as if to say, "Let's get out of here."

Michael gave her a cool half smile and returned his full attention to Nicole.

For Jo, it was an invitation. All she had to do was find the means. And it seemed as if his partner, who was a fair dancer, would be pretty easy to conquer. After all, she was a little older, and redheads were so common anymore. Jo was determined by whatever means, she would get the woman out of the picture.

"Friend of yours?" Nicole asked Michael.

"No, but you know everyone knows everyone here. Jo is a few years younger than you. Grew up in Upland, graduated, and works at the Quick Mart. She certainly can dance."

"She certainly believes she can- as do many others."

Michael stumbled for a second, frowned, and then shrugged his shoulders good-naturedly, "It comes naturally to some and not to others."

"Want to cool down?" she asked.

"Am I that bad?"

"Not at all. I want to talk to you without you having to watch your back and mine."

Michael laughed, unleashing a deep booming sound that Nicole found very pleasing. "Let's go outside for a few minutes."

The pair went out and found a short wall that was unoccupied and sat on it.

"So, what did you want to talk about?" Michael asked.

"Lena came over with a story that was a little incredulous." Nicole explained, and she told him the whole story. "And that is how we ended up here." she finished.

"Look, I sit the fence on things like this. I have seen the reality of death on the road, in houses, from people who were supposed to love you and those who obviously didn't. I believe there is a release of the human spirit. And in death, who knows what happens to it. There is no denying your house is creepy."

"How would you know?"

"It holds bad vibes from your childhood. That much is clear. Do I believe your parents haunt the house? I think their spirits are still there in some form. Call it a ghost, pent-up energy, whatever. But what is Lena suggesting... not one but two premonitions were designed to show two people were going to be killed?"

"This conversation is thirsty work."

"I could use a cold drink." Michael said.

More or less dancing themselves to their table, they noticed the lack of wait staff and Lena's absence. "I'll go get our drinks. What would you like?" Michael asked.

"Just water. I need to clear out the rest of this alcohol."

Michael made his way to the bar. Jo detached herself from the throng on the floor and made her way to the bar as well.   " A r e you with the woman you were dancing with? The one whose parents were killed?"

"We're enjoying the evening together."

"You could use a little help on the dance floor. I'd be happy to help."

"You want to teach me to dance?"

She stood up and whispered to him, "Sure, I've been told I have some good moves."

"I'm sure you do, but I don't think I'd have time."

"Then maybe we could just get together?"

"I don't know. I am pretty busy."

"I like challenges." She placed a perfumed card in his pocket. "Anytime, anyplace."

"Don't wait up for me."

She smiled, displaying beautifully white and even teeth. "Text me, and I will be glad to get back to you as soon as possible."

Michael shook his head as she watched her sway her way back to the waiting throng of admirers. Did anyone really think those come-on tactics worked?

As he waited for the drinks, he read her card.

JO DE BEAUVOIR

Massage and

Deep Relaxation Meditation

765-555-JO4U

@jo4u

Her address was local, and so was the number. Michael smiled and tucked the card in his back pocket. He made a note to check out her business veracity.

TWENTY-ONE

When he returned to their table, Nicole looked amused.

"What?" Looking around, Michael saw a bunch of people who seemed so much unlike himself. He liked a good time, and god knows he did his share of partying until he graduated from the police academy. He never felt like he fit in with the crowd before him. Work hard, play hard, drink hard was the motto around these parts. Now, he still liked a good time, but he always had too much of a sense of responsibility.

Much like Nicole. From the time she was in high school, she was serious and dedicated to whatever she put her mind to. She had been dealt shit where her parents were concerned, and yet, she was able to go to school and build a business. That took guts, dedication, and responsibility, despite the money she had.

"Did you turn her down?" Nicole asked teasingly.

"I am here, aren't I? I am old-fashioned. I like to leave with the person who brought me."

"So you're leaving alone?"

"Do you have a better offer?" he mischievously grinned. Clearly, tonight Nicole was putting some of that responsibility and seriousness on hold, but she hadn't changed from that girl he knew as she graduated high school. She listened to him, she was so bright, and he knew how beautiful she was. So beautiful, it made his cock throb just thinking about her. Beyond his boner, he knew she was special.

Nicole looked him up and down, "Maybe. But what are we going to do about her?" She motioned to Lena, who was now out on the floor, giving Jo a run for her money.

"Judging from the way things are going, I think Lena may be spending the night somewhere else."

Nicole looked at the dance floor. Instead of competing, Jo and Lena seemed to have joined forces and were bumping and grinding each other with their followers flocked around them in a protective herd. Nicole nodded to Lena indicating she was leaving. Lena smiled her response and continued dancing.

Nicole looked at Michael, "Let's go."

When they arrived at her house, he carried her inside and laid her gently on the bed. Slowly and with punctuating kisses, he removed her clothing, piece by piece. Once she was naked and he could look at her in her glorious entirety, he kissed her from head to toe, languidly stroking her skin with his hands, lips, and tongue.

Finally, he paused to remove his own clothes. Delightedly Nicole watched as arms, legs, ass, stomach, and cock appeared for her to drink in.

"I remember something like this in a field once," Nicole commented.

"Uh-hmm." He kissed her forehead, her cheeks, and her lips.

"Although I was somewhat more tentative then."

Michael stopped and looked at her, "Oh, and you have so much more experience now?"

"Like you haven't been with anyone since the pond."

"Well..." he trailed off.

Her eyes flew open, "Don't tell me you haven't been with anyone."

"I'm selective."

"And I'm not? What exactly are you saying?" Nicole sat up.

He stroked her arm, "I'm saying, I have

only been with one other person since you. It was a six-month relationship. We parted on good terms."

"And does she live around here?" Nicole demanded.

Michael laughed, "Did I ask you where your old boyfriends lived?"

"Well, seeing as Lane is dead, it doesn't matter. And the other guy was a one-nighter." Seeing Michael's face, "I blew off some steam." Seeing his skeptical face, she continued, "I was safe. I have never had a one-night stand before that. I've been too busy working. It was a kickoff to a relaxing vacation." She snorted, some vacation.

Michael moved to get up, "I forgot..."

Nicole stopped him, "I've got you covered this time." She opened her nightstand drawer and pulled out a handful of condoms. "As memory serves, we went through four of these in an afternoon. Are you still up for that, or should I put some back?" Nicole's eyes twinkled.

Michael took in the contents of the drawer. "Hmmm, it appears your one-nighter didn't make an excellent night of it with you after all."

"Who says this was the box we used?"

Nicole laughed.

The next few hours were familiar, new, and exciting. Familiar because they had been together before. New because they had both had lovers and matured since their first times. Exciting because it was mutual giving and taking.

Nicole rolled Michael onto his back and loved over his body. She started by looking into his eyes and stroking his hair. Kissing him brought back so many memories, good memories of their earlier times. She still found the warm younger man who showed her such consideration in the field underneath the maturity.

She moved down, her mouth playing over his nipples; she rubbed her face over his broader chest and reached down to grasp his cock. "This feels as hard as ever."

Michael throatily laughed, "As I said, your one nighter-"

Nicole squeezed him, "My one-nighter was only that. A one-nighter."

"And me? Am I a one-nighter?"

Nicole smiled as she dipped her head lower, "This is our second round." She licked his shaft like a candy cane. He smelled so good, so familiar and musky. Nicole sucked his cock head, tasting Michael.

She couldn't stop herself; she was surprised at how wet and throbbing she was. Nicole straddled Michael and held his hands. Slowly, she rode him, moving up and down and circling her hips.

He detached their hands and squeezed her bottom, and she moved. A long moan escaped his lips, and she smiled, resting her hands on his chest. She moved faster, stroking her clitoris with the shaft of his cock. Her long hair fell over her shoulders, and she felt her orgasm coming as she watched him below her, rasping and moaning. His fingers dug into her hips.

They looked at each other, their eyes locked. Michael's gray eyes bore into hers as she unapologetically came over his cock, finally throwing her head back and yelling.

As her aftershocks subsided, he smiled, "Are you ready for another go? He's still got life in him."

"Just try me." Nicole said.

Michael laughed and, in one motion, pulled her under him. He looked into her eyes again and thrust deeply into her. On his knees, Michael pumped in and out, withdrawing completely and thrusting deeply back in. He rested on his forearms, tugging her nipples with his soft lips, and punctuating each plunge with a grunt.

Nicole spread her legs wide, "I can't get enough of you," she rasped in his ear.

"Then I guess we aren't just a fling," he murmured, feeling his balls tighten at her voice in his ear.

"I want to feel you cum inside me," she whispered. "I want to feel you cum deep inside me. You feel so good, so big,"

He rolled to his right side, bringing Nicole with him. He pulled her right leg over his shoulder and pushed inside her to his balls. And he paused.

Michael looked at Nicole. "You feel so good around me. You are so beautiful."

She looked at him, feeling him fill her.

Nicole squirmed, trying to get some stimulation, "You! You are so mean." she laughed when he moved, leaving only his tip inside.

He kissed her forehead, nose, and lips and watched her eyes close in pleasure as he once again thrust inside her.

Pumping slowly, Michael reached down

and stroked Nicole's clitoris like a tiny cock. His left held her ass close to him.

Her eyes flew open as he stroked her tiny button. She moaned so loudly until the room was filled with her voice, and he felt her tighten and thrust with him.

Listening to her, Michael could go on no more, and he exploded inside her, his body quivering and quaking over and over.

He looked at Nicole. Her eyes were still closed, and he felt her sheath contracting still. Her breath was ragged, and a bead of sweat rolled between her breasts.

Michael leaned his head down and licked up the trace moisture. Nicole opened her eyes.

"So," she teased, "Is that all you've got?"

"You have no idea what I've got. But you will."

The figure in the corner of the room watched the pair with hatred. It made a plan to take care of both of them.

TWENTY-TWO

Nicole cursed the long path up to the house. Too much for one person to snow blow. For the past two hours, Nicole had been trying to make a path out to the road. It had been almost impossible to get out of the house, but she wanted to give it a try anyway.

The night Michael spent with her, it began to snow. He was called in, and it had been snowing ever since. Twenty-four hours later, almost a foot of snow dropped. It was great to be alone, but Lena came back as soon as the roads were clear.

And with a prediction of eight more inches, it meant Lena wasn't going anywhere. Rideshares were limiting the types of rides and areas their drivers worked, and due to travel advisories, no one was permitted a long drive. Lena should have been back at her apartment in Indianapolis.

Lena shot out of the house bundled in Nicole's coat and a pair of Nicole's boots.

So happy to see she could make herself at home, Nicole thought. "What's happened to you? You look like you've met a ghost."

"I have," Lena choked out. Her hands were shaking as she clicked her vape pen.

Nicole's patience was wearing thin. "What is going on?"

"You tell me."

"Lena-" Nicole warned.

"You're house is haunted."

"You know, after my parents died, everyone said this house was haunted. Hell, they said that before. You know better than anyone."

"I do, and that is why I swore I would never set foot in here again." Lena toked nervously on her vape pen.

Nicole studied Lena.

She was shaking.

This behavior was slumber party level.

Nicole almost believed her.

"Look, this house is cheerless and unhappy. For whatever reason, it doesn't like me. And just now, I came face to face with your father."

Nicole shrugged, "It doesn't surprise me. I hear mom more than dad. I need to cleanse the house-"

"He came around the corner after I went to the bathroom, and he laughed at me."

Again, Nicole shrugged, "I didn't hear it,

but it sounds like something he would do. He was always trying to scare us."

Lena shook her head vigorously, "You don't understand. He laughed so, so, evilly. And then he drew his finger over his throat, pointed at me, and laughed."

Nicole stood silently.

With no tangible response from Nicole, Lena rolled her eyes. "T'ohhhhh! I can't stand being stuck here! I'm going for a walk."

"Lena, the snow is over a foot deep in some places, And it is freezing."

"But it is sunny, and the snow is starting to melt. Besides, I am not staying in that house by myself again."

"I have work to do out here. And there is a chance of more snow today." Nicole reminded her.

"Only a thirty percent chance," Lena grumbled.

"Oh fine, go out." Nicole said crossly. "I am going to salt the driveway so we can keep up with any additional snow." The truth was that she was developing cabin fever as well. The one time, she didn't have loads of work piled up for her to do, and she could not enjoy it. The contractors had canceled until after the roads were passable. She'd checked in with her office, and they said to enjoy her vacation.

Nicole also had other more important things to do. She had already worked with the State of Indiana to convert the Gutzwillers' property to a Freiwald, a cemetery in which cremains are put into biodegradable containers, buried next to existing or new trees. It seemed a lucrative business, depending on how deep remains needed to be and how many sets of ashes would be allowed around trees. It was also a cheap alternative to caskets and the whole rigmarole. She had done a virtual conference call with the State Board of Funeral and Cemetery Services to plead her case. It looked good.

And honestly, Lena was not helping. She bitched about the snow, and she couldn't stop talking about all the weird stuff that happened in the house, Lane's death, and how badly she was sleeping. And Jo.

"You would think with your money you'd have a heated driveway to this old house," Lena grumbled.

"And you'd think arriving unannounced and spouting shit that anyone else would call you crazy for would make you a little less of a bitch. But here we are."

Nicole sighed, somewhat contrite, "Be sure to layer your clothes. It is still cold. You know how it gets around here."

"Yes, Mom." Lena sang.

Nicole looked pointedly at Lena. "Be careful."

TWENTY-THREE

Sandalwood incense and vanilla musk candles were the combinations Jeremy Charrier found winning to most women. And during his night flights, it was the same. It helped him relax and go to a good place mentally while traveling to do whatever business he had. It was also a combination his current client adored.

Jeremy was not the most brilliant person in the world; he knew that. He was, nevertheless, crafty as hell. And that meant finding ways to make his lot work for him.

Tarot cards had been his first gig and still were part of his bread and butter to keep up appearances. Next came dating the girl who was into astral projection. He thought of it as another hoop to get laid. Now, it was his key to whatever he wanted.

Lately, however, he'd hit a snag. His tarot readings were all dark, which was concerning and unusual. At first, when it happened, he blew it off. You always have some dark material to manage with clients. But more and more clients were having death and hardships dealt to them by the cards. It led to some heavy manipulation and interpretation.

Today, he pursed his lips and gently stroked the cards with his fingertips. He alternated between looking at the cards and closing his eyes thoughtfully before presenting his findings. Occasionally, he would wrinkle his brown in circumspection as if trying to squeeze more information from the cards. Then he would stroke the cards again with a nod of satisfaction.

His tools included a round table covered with a thick gold velvet tablecloth fringed in cream. His signature incense and the recorded gentle sound of rain and crashes of thunder wafted around the room.

Across the table from Jeremy sat Mr. Gingham. He was middle-aged but tried to look younger with his tonics, creams, and anything short of a face-lift, which was quickly going to be in his future, judging from the crow's feet at the corners of his eyes and their luggage hanging under his eyes.

Mr. Gingham watched Jeremy keenly, his expressions ebbing and flowing with Jeremy's own practiced looks. He watched Jeremy's hands and nervously stroked the table cloth lightly. Chewing his lower lip to a thin, bloody line, Mr. Gingham's breathing came shallow and fast.

"And there we have it," Jeremy said, at last, wiping his brow with the silk handkerchief he always kept on the table as a show of the physical toll each reading took on him.

Mr. Gingham leaned forward and contemplated the cards. "What's the good word, Jeremy?"

Jeremy moved his hand from side to side. "The next week or so is somewhat in conflict. But in two weeks, your news should be what you desire."

"My business is expanding," Mr. Gingham's face lit up, and he licked his abused lips.

"Until then," Jeremy warned, "Watch for people around you spreading lies."

"Who is it?" Mr. Gingham eagerly asked.

Jeremy closed his eyes, "The cards cannot tell us that, but I am getting a name that starts with S. S-E-something...." He chose two of the most used letters of the alphabet.

"Sean." Mr. Gingham said with disgust. "I knew he was no good. He is one of the managers opposed to company growth."

Jeremy looked back to the cards, "Yes,

yes, I can see that in this card. The reversed Emperor. He lives in tyranny, and your changes would usurp that."

"Can you tell me more?"

Jeremy reflected on the upright cards. "Here, the reversed Hermit and upright Strength. These are representative of you. You are strong but in danger of losing your way due to the Emperor." *Poor bastard Sean*, Jeremy thought, *but someone had to be the fall guy.*

"We will see about that," Mr. Gingham harrumphed.

"Justice is upright, meaning you will triumph in the end."

Mr. Gingham giggled like a naughty child. "Indeed, I will. What else can you tell me?"

Jeremy touched his brow and sighed, "The veil is closing. That is all I can tell you today." He paused for a few moments, wiped his brow again, and asked brightly, "Same time in two weeks?"

"Of course, Jeremy. Without your guidance, I would be lost."

Jeremy assumed a humble expression. "If in my small way, I can help make your path clear, then I am happy."

"Thank you again, Jeremy."

Jeremy removed the cards and straightened the tablecloth.

"Before I go, Jeremy, would it be possible to get a cup of that lovely herbal tea and a cake pop?"

Jeremy moved his expression to sorrowful, "Alas, I am out of my herbal tea. My supplier has been unable to get that blend for me but has promised it will be here next week. I'll save you some."

Jeremy's herbal tea dealer was really himself, and he was waiting for a new crop to mature. He would steep it in water, throw in a bit of butter for the THC to stick to, and strain the lot. Then he would add a little lemon juice and cinnamon to balance out the taste. It was also the secret ingredient in his cake pops.

"What a pity. But until next time."

Usually, Jeremy wouldn't have a problem watching Mr. Gingham get high on a cuppa and cake pops. For what he paid for his bogus sessions, Jeremy could afford to indulge the occasional customer. And spiked tea and cake were much easier on him than the special services some of his other clients requested. But Jeremy did whatever he needed to and did not complain. He kept many secrets, and in turn, he was kept in money, cars, and clothes.

Today was a little different. Jeremy wanted to get Mr. Gingham out so that he could speak with Nicole. When she called him out of the blue, he was frankly surprised. They had been friendly enough while he was dating her sister but didn't really connect.

She was young and attractive and not at all his clientele. He occasionally guessed right and correctly sensed Nicole had something otherworldly to discuss.

He accompanied Mr. Gingham to the door and watched him descend the stairs to his classic Camaro. He waved as he donned his aviator sunglasses and pulled out of the winding drive. The metal doors clinked shut, and Jeremy stood on the balcony, breathing in the fresh air.

This area was perfect for his needs. At night, the events he held were enhanced by the Victorian landscape. The long drive took visitors through a maze of purposely planted vegetation, setting the mood long before they arrived at the towering Gothic Revival home. In each section, astrological and other occult symbolatry decorated the paths. Nestled amongst the shrubs were good luck charms and evil-warders. Enough to suggest mystery and give him credibility, but not too much to frighten his clients.

The windows were high and arched, with decorative molding above each of them. The mansard-roofed tower exhibited the same rounded windows and bargeboard along the edges.

Inside, the home's fourteen-foot ceilings made rooms seem enormous, while the ornate Victorian furniture made the rooms seem like a home. Only the downstairs where customers sat was decorated so heavily. Upstairs, everything was very modern.

Back inside, he found he had a few minutes to kill before Nicole arrived. He changed the music to classic rock. Listening for a moment, he nodded his approval. Not too pushy. *Just in case,* he told himself.

He brought out a little wine to let it breathe. Let Nicole decide if she wanted something harder. She called him, and he was happy to have her take the lead.

Life had not always been fair to Jeremy. Graduating with a killer girlfriend had been bad enough, but after graduation was even worse. The people of the town looked at him with a mix of curiosity and suspicion. It was all they wanted to talk about. Dating a killer, dating the girl who had killed her parents. Even after leaving the Cheers, as Jeremy called Upland, he had difficulty finding a supply of bread. Even though everyone didn't know his name in Indianapolis, he went through a series of dead-end jobs and moved in with roommates to make ends meet. One was a writer and the other into the theater.

Both men were gay as the day was long; he tagged along to the endless parties they were invited to. As a young and attractive man, this invariably led to other invitations. And as someone who loved to eat and had no money, this was the best way of getting food without paying for it.

He found out quickly that being a boy toy for a gay man wasn't the way he wanted to go. He had no problem with anyone and who they did or didn't do. It just wasn't his thing. So he developed a specialty that could be dragged out in an instant at parties.

Jeremy started with palmistry and then moved to empath skills. When women or men heard, "You've survived some pretty intense things in recent years all by yourself," who could resist the flattery. Soon, Jeremy found himself invited to straight parties and increasingly, parties hosted by patrons of the arts, a.k.a., money.

And the money he made. It started with tips, then real money for his antics. The more he schmoozed, the more they begged for his services, in and out of the bedroom. Before long, he had his Victorian home, paid for by some of the choicest tail in the state. Now, he was one of the most sought-after mediums in North America, and he was building a clientele across the ocean as well. He was available by referral only to keep him exclusive. His life allowed him to travel when he wanted it. And Renee no longer haunted his life.

Which brought him back to Nicole. He didn't usually have to work hard for his conquests. And she would be an interesting one. Lena may have brought her back into his life due to her incessant need to one-up Nicole, but for the time being, he was patient enough to listen to whatever she had to say so he could ultimately get in her pants for a financial payoff. After all, with her career shining, he doubted she would want a first-hand account of her sister on the tabloid newsstand.

TWENTY-FOUR

The young women were finally asleep. It was bad enough with the horrible family who lived in the home, but the young misses cackling like chickens till all indecent hours got on his nerves. It was like the shrill sound of cannon fire.And the topic was always young men.

Corporal Jacob Wolverton grabbed his gun and loaded it. An intruder was in his home. *Bastard Mexicans.* He'd had enough of them during the War. At Molino del Rey, the Americans had won, but only after the Mexicans fired on their own forces. He'd been lucky and only took a bullet in the shoulder, but half his company died, and he was the only survivor from his squad.

He snapped a bayonet onto the gun. *I'll be damned if those dark-haired twin vipers are going to camp out in my home.* The younger one was most definitely a whore. They were corrupting the other girls. Defiling his home.

They needed to go. A taste of his musket might help.

"¡Madre de Dios! ¡Un fantasma! ¡Madre

de Dios! Madre de Dios!"

Nicole sleepily opened her eyes. "What's going on?" She looked at the commotion around her. All the girls were awake. Lena was screaming in Spanish. "What is she saying?"

Laurel answered, "She is saying 'Mother of God. A ghost.'"

Nicole's eyes flew open. That was the last thing they needed. "Are you sure it wasn't my mom or dad walking through?"

"No!" Lena snapped, "It wasn't. It was a soldier in a cape with a gun and bayonet. And he was standing in front of me, glaring at me, and pointing the bayonet at me!"

Nicole couldn't believe her ears. Nicole and Renee saw him a year ago, but he seemed more curious than vengeful. But for someone else besides Renee to experience paranormal activity in the house gave her the knowledge that she wasn't crazy. Her dad swore he never experienced anything and her mom only believed in the Holy Ghost.

"Let's get back to sleep." Coro suggested.

"No!" screeched Lena. "I want to go home. I know what I saw!"

By this time, Dee was up. She sighed deeply. She was pissed that her sleep had been interrupted. "Get your things together. I will call your parents."

The rest of the girls went back to sleep, but the damage was done.

In the end, Lindsey drove Lena and Jackie home.

When the girls woke up much later, aside from wondering if Lena was ok, it was a subdued post-party. Shortly after breakfast, Dee conveyed the other girls home, declaring after the last had left the car that they would never have another group over again. Nicole and Renee looked at each other dejectedly.

That day they spent the day in church. Back at home, the mood was not much better. Their father was pissed because of his missed sleep and took it out on their mother. The girls stayed out of their way, only coming downstairs to use the bathroom and a monosyllabic dinner.

Up in Nicole's room, they talked. Nicole said, "If the soldier was old enough, he could have had an issue with Spanish people. You know, the Spanish-American war?"

"Then why wasn't Jackie targeted?"

Nicole shrugged, "Maybe he picked the weaker link? It got them both out of the house."

Renee shook her head, "I don't know, but

Lena was adamant about what she saw. Did you hear her Spanish?"

"I know! They never speak Spanish with us!"

School didn't help cushion the situation. Lena made sure the word got around, and it fractured the friends. Only Coro would speak with Nicole and Renee, which was only because she didn't believe in ghosts. Even Jackie said she couldn't talk with her anymore. "My parents think the devil is at your house."

Their invitations to other houses and parties dried up, and the sisters felt the loss keenly. The flipside was that Renee caught Jeremy Charrier's eye, who was deeply interested in the paranormal.

For Nicole, she felt very alone. And she threw herself into her schoolwork, earning good grades. While the smart set respected her intellect, she still had no close friends.

Until she met Michael Madigan.

TWENTY-FIVE

Nicole's bike wound its way up the winding pathway, the sound of the engine echoing through the quiet landscape. Jeremy did have one of the finest pieces of property in Indianapolis. It sat on a small bluff overlooking the White River. The snow abated and quickly melted with the return of the warm temperatures. Nicole called Jeremy, and he said he would squeeze her in.

She stopped in front of the impressive mansion at sunset and suddenly got a "what the fuck am I doing" feeling. Nicole was familiar with the feeling. When she took a leap of faith, like with her business or college, it was understandable. But this? Still, she felt like she must be losing her mind.

Nicole wished Michael was joining her. Spending time with him made her feel happy, cheerful, and safe. Nicole realized that when she started school, and since then, she'd so missed his friendship, and they had been friends. For months they talked, fooled around, and because she went to school, it stopped. Michael had gone his way, and Nicole went hers. She went back to the pond several times, but he was never there. And she didn't have the nerve to contact him.

First, Lena shows up with some cock and bull story. Then she leaves a note saying she is going out with Jo. During the middle of a snow event. Nicole assumed she was still with Jo as she still hadn't come back for her things.

Now she felt compelled to talk to Jeremy, her psycho sister's boyfriend and one of Lena's many conquests. Nicole knew that ghosts were real, but what seemed to be going on went beyond that. Coupled with Lena's weird questions... Nicole reminded herself that is why she was here.

She did some research on him online, and out of everyone she knew, Jeremy was the one who knew the most about the occult. Or at least this was the one that Nicole wanted to start with because she was at least familiar with. Nicole knew part of his living was a schtick, but surely he knew something that might be able to help her sort things out.

"Welcome, come on in," he greeted her warmly, opening the door for her. He was dressed in a priest's frock coat and matching black pants. Expensive European shoes covered his feet, and his hair was impeccably styled in a faded pompadour undercut. His bright blue eyes bored into hers.

The room he brought her to was large by any standards and filled with floor-to-ceiling built-in cabinets filled with all sorts of occult objects. Crystal balls, cards, dice, mirrors, pendulums, books, and more filled the space. The furniture was comfortable Victorian furniture fashionably updated in bright steampunk shades.

"Did you have problems finding the place?" he asked.

"Not at all. I love to explore places, so I am pretty familiar with this area. I didn't know you lived up here, though."

"It's a great area." He gestured to the bottle on the coffee table. "What can I get you? Wine? I was about to have a glass."

"That would be great." Nicole sat on the purple velvet Eastlake settee.

Jeremy plopped next to her and handed her a generous glass of wine.

"I hope I am not bothering you…" Nicole trailed off. She took a long drink of the red liquid.

"Not at all, not at all. I don't have another

client for," Jeremy glanced at the clock, "a couple hours. Now, what can I do for you? It sounded urgent."

"I am not exactly sure what I want from you. Things are happening, I don't understand all of them, and since you knew Renee and were into the occult..."

"We were into astral projection and the hauntings in your house. Not the occult."

Nicole shrugged her shoulders. "Maybe there is nothing you can do for me."

Jeremy shook his head, inhaling almost half his glass of wine. "Don't be so sure. Just tell me what is going on."

"Long story short, my parents haunt my house. You, of all people, know my parents weren't stellar people. They play pranks and all, but I just leave them there. I didn't believe until now that they could really influence anything."

"What do you feel like they are influencing?"

"They are not just turning on televisions and lights anymore. They are talking. And they are scaring the people who come into my house."

"How so?"

Nicole shifted her eyes and took another

deep drag of her wine. "They are appearing to my guests. And I will eventually have business people in the house. If it were just that, I would say just get rid of them and be done."

"But there is something else, right? Something that doesn't fit with them?" Jeremy had a bad feeling about what she was going to say.

"Yes. There is something far more sinister than my parents in the house- if that is even possible. Until now, they were just mildly annoying. Now, it is like there is someone else. I don't know. Watching and commenting." She told him about Lena's experience in her house.

"Do you have any ideas who it is?" This was a deviation from the plan, but that was Lena. He'd roll with it.

"None at all. But it isn't good. It is, well, sinister."

Jeremy studied Nicole. "And that made you call me?"

Nicole finished her wine, and Jeremy swooped in with the bottle to refill her ample cup. "Not exactly. I just know that you taught Renee about things, and maybe in your experience," Nicole stressed the word, "That you have some idea about what is going on.

Lena also mentioned you didn't think that her experience with seeing my sister could have been anything."

That's what he was waiting for. He promised Lena he would lead Nicole down a path to make Lena feel better about herself. Whatever it took to keep her quiet and the pussy coming.

"I told Lena there was no way any path in the occult short of death would allow Renee to be in two places at once. I think she has many demons, and maybe she has some sort of unfinished business that keeps intruding in her dreams. After all, Lena was your friend and your sisters in high school. I remember you and your friends had a break in your friendship. Maybe that's it. As for the rest, true, I work with the unknown. I act as a guide for whatever people need help with. Have you been doing anything in the house? Rituals? Incantations? Construction?"

Nicole frowned, "Construction? What does that have to do with it?"

Jeremy leaned back and downed his own glass. Now, he was getting somewhere. "Energy is energy. It never goes away; it only changes forms. So when you die, your energy just changes form. Additionally, some people believe that organic things hold vibrations of the past and that disturbing those organic things releases the spirit energy."

"Organic? Like natural and cage-free?"

Jeremy laughed, the winemaking him more loquacious than usual. He refilled his own glass, "No, organic like dirt, wood, and other things that occur in nature."

"So you think the construction I am going to do on my house is causing this? How can this be the cause if I haven't started? The dirt-moving, the dust unsettled, the wood added? This activity might be upsetting the spirits in my house?"

"Construction is one possibility. The talk of it and the spirits aware of it is another. They are just like us, only dead."

Nicole nodded, "Ok, I can get behind that. My parents are examples of that. They got pissed when I went to college. My mom banged around the house and said things like I would never make it. My dad would smoke- I smelled his cigarettes. And make an occasional comment about how I was wasting time." She considered the conversation for a moment. "What other possibilities are there?

Like I said, my parents have only ever been annoying. What I am feeling is palpable. Like it could almost be touched."

"You could have brought something into the house, or you could have disturbed something that was already there but not activated. An old ghost soul, so to speak. Or it could be a transient spirit on its way to somewhere else or goes where it wants."

"Will sage and sweetgrass be enough to cleanse the house and restore balance? I've done that for years. I am going to be doing quite a bit of construction on-site over the next few months."

Jeremy shrugged, "It depends. It may take more than one cleansing. If you want, I can come over and take a look." *Easy.*

"Do you think it might help?"

"Oh, I definitely think it will help."

TWENTY-SIX

The window was open, and the sweet smell of fresh air drifted in and mingled with the honeyed musk of sex that no amount of science could reproduce.

Nicole rolled over in her large bed and nuzzled Michael Madigan's bare shoulder and chest.

He kissed the top of her head, "Comfortable?"

"Uh-huh. I don't want to leave this bed."

"We might need to before Mrs. Tenant comes. Or we need food. Or I have to go to work."

Nicole groaned. "What time is it?"

Michael reached for his cell phone and brought it closer to see it.

"Five o'clock."

"A.M or P.M?"

"P.M."

"Damn, that means that you'll have to work soon." Nicole said.

"Too soon."

Nicole looked into Michael's eyes, "Do you realize we spent the last twenty-four hours in bed?"

"Not true!" Michael countered, "We ordered food, we went downstairs to get it, and I did investigate that weird window that broke. And we talked about Lena and her issues. And this house's issues."

"True. But I don't want to talk about Lena. Or the strange happenings in this house. I still don't know how that window broke."

"Lena is full of shit like always. I am sure she has an angle. And yes, your house seems to have a lot of unexplained activity. But it is all explainable. Stress, old house issues, nerves. And the window was old, and the expansion and contraction of the window frame finally cracked it."

Nicole rubbed her hand over Michael's lovely blossom of soft chest hair, his flat tummy with the delicious path of hair to his narrow hips and...

"Are you looking for trouble?" He asked.

"I think I already found it," she said, bending over to suck the tip of his penis.

"Hey, hey, hey..." Michael rolled over to face her. They looked deeply into each other's eyes. He kissed her cheeks, forehead, and lips. She returned the kiss, her mouth open and eager.

His hand moved down over the smooth curves of her back and rested on her bottom. She could feel his excitement pressing against her silky thighs. Nicole opened her legs. Michael ran his hand over the arch of her hip and slid into the dampness between her legs.

Nicole gasped as Michael's strong fingers stroked her, darting in and out of her wetness and returning to the throbbing button nestled between her lips. Pushing against his hand, she moaned her approval, sucking his tongue as they locked lips.

He removed the sheet that had tangled between them and shifted position. Nicole reached to guide him into her, looking deep into his eyes. She could feel the throb of the big vein that ran the length of his long, hard cock.

Michael rolled on top of her, and she pulled him to her. Gently, he stoked her fire, alternating between kissing her soft lips and the berry tips of her rounded breasts. He stroked in and then out as he felt her wetness tighten around him. His breath grew ragged, and his movements gradually became more insistent and tigerish as their climax approached. She cried out in release as wave after wave of orgasm hit her.

Hearing her mews of pleasure unmanned him, and he poured his release into her. They clung to each other, chests heaving, sweat soaking each other, coming to a slow shuddering quiet. Nicole pressed her legs together to hold him inside just a while longer.

"I love you, Nicole," he whispered.

"I love you, too." she found herself saying.

They looked at each other for what seemed like hours. And they kissed again.

"So... what do we do now?" Nicole asked softly.

"Go with it." And kissed her again.

TWENTY-SEVEN

Nicole wondered how they had arrived at the dark situation they were in. True to his dubious word, Jeremy came over and did a walk-through of her house. He told her that there were a lot of angry spirits in the house. None of them seemed to be directing their anger at her, but they definitely wanted her attention. Jeremy offered to come out to do a seance to see what he could find.

Jeremy whistled as he got ready for his evening. He primped an extra time in the mirror, being sure every crack and crevice was powered and scented just in case he got lucky. The seance would work to his advantage. He would make sure of it. He didn't get to this point in his career by taking big chances. And to get lucky with a piece like Nicole was just icing he couldn't resist.

When he did the walk-through during the day, he didn't notice much out of the ordinary- at first. Everyone knew the house was haunted, and he didn't disagree. He did feel a lot of negative energy, but given that two ghosts were Nicole's parents, who never liked him anyway, it didn't surprise him.

Driving in the light rain, Jeremy hoped he was successful. When he arrived for the seance that evening, he was less happy to see Michael Madigan at the house. Still, it didn't matter. Jeremy was sure he could keep up the pretense and make something convincing to get him an invitation back.

"Where is Lena?" Jeremy asked.

Nicole shrugged, "She left to visit Jo de Beauvoir, someone she met when we were at the High Tunnel a few days ago. She hasn't called me. Her stuff is still here."

Jeremy was not pleased Lena was slacking on this plan of hers, but he could make this work. Lena didn't have a lot going for her in terms of money or common sense, but she knew how to network, no matter by what means she accomplished it. Lena had good contacts that Jeremy could use, and for that alone, he continued on with the act.

The three sat in a circle on the living room floor. White candles graced the furniture, and Jeremy began to explain the process. "While we hold hands, I will try to connect with the spirits. They may speak through me or," he looked at the pair, "they may choose to speak through you. Whatever you do, whatever happens, do not attempt to stop the interaction or the spirit may be trapped here."

"What happens if the spirit is trapped here?" Nicole asked. "I thought they could go wherever whenever. That's why my parents don't show themselves all the time. Or at least that's what I thought."

"That is generally true, but if they have been summoned and the channel not properly closed, they could be forced to stay here."

"Couldn't you just close the channel by rejoining hands and speaking?" Michael sardonically queried.

"Sometimes that works, but their residual energy could cause issues. Like a residual haunting." Jeremy spouted what he read in the books.

The two men sat with Nicole between them. "Now, close your eyes." Jeremy began, "Dear spirits in this home, please tell us why you want to communicate with Nicole. Please let us know how we can help you."

They waited silently.

"Spirits, speak freely to or through us. We want to hear you and to help you."

They all heard a sound like breaking glass.

"Stay where you are." Jeremy commanded Nicole and Michael. To the spirits he said, "We hear you. Who are you? How can we help you?"

A breeze surrounded the group. "Do you feel that?" Nicole asked.

"It is just the spirit communicating." Jeremy indicated. He would thank Luis, his man of all jobs, for the broken window and the added breeze. What a genius move!

They heard a voice. "Nicole? It's Lane."

"Lane?" Nicole asked.

"Nicole, watch out. She's coming for you."

The breeze changed, and something oddly familiar was in the air.

"Sables and Pearls." Nicole said, "Renee wore it all the time." Her brow wrinkled, "But how could it be hers?" She isn't dead."

"Residual energy." I will have to thank Luis. Works like a charm every time.

Renee, Dee, and Lindsey appeared. Dee spoke accusingly, "What are you doing home so early? If you got expelled, so help me..." She put down the iced tea.

"I'm going to take care of you and dad once and for all," Renee replied.

Her father's voice boomed in the crashing thunder-like way he did when he was angry.

"What the hell are you talking about?" He was sitting in the kitchen drinking coffee and smoking a Salem.

"This." Renee put the gun to his chest and pulled the trigger. A shot fired, causing the group to open their eyes. Before them, they saw Lindsey on the ground, blood cascading from the massive wound.

Renee turned to her mother. "You never cared about me. You never cared that he fucked his own daughter or her daughter's friends."

"You're insane." Dee taunted. "She pulled her long-nailed hand back and brought it down on Renee's arm."

"Better insane than dead, you spineless bitch." Renee slapped her hand away, grabbed her arm, and pulled her close. Renee fired again. She watched her mother fall and spit on both bodies. She looked at the spot where her mother's fingernails went through her skin. Hopefully, the flight kept fingerprints from sticking. She dropped the gun.

The group watched as Renee floated upward. The whole scene disappeared.

Suddenly, the same laughter she heard earlier pealed over their heads. It seemed to come from all around them.

"Go in peace, spirit, go in peace. Be gone from this house, I rebuke you!" Jeremy intoned with more conviction than he felt. *This was not part of the gag.*

The laughter culminated into a frenzy of crazy rifts and intelligible mumbling.

The candles levitated, rocking and spilling wax.

A blood-curdling scream sounded.

"I rebuke you. Leave this house!" Jeremy repeated.

The candles dropped, and the voice stopped.

Jeremy broke the circle. "Turn on the lights."

Nicole turned on the lights, "What the hell was that? Did you hear what she said about my dad? My friends?"

"One thing at a time. I am going to find out what the hell it was." Michael left the room.

Jeremy was a little stunned. This was not part of the plan.

Michael reappeared shortly with a small bottle. "What is the real deal behind this?"

Nicole looked at the bottle of Sales and Pearls in disbelief. She looked at Jeremy.

Damn that bean eater; why did he leave

that perfume out? Jeremy chuckled nervously, "Ok, I was trying to make it interesting."

"Oh, it's interesting, alright. Your friend is out there- dead." Michael accused.

After the initial shock wore off, Jeremy begged him not to call the police, "I can't have my business wrapped in murder."

But his plea fell on deaf ears. The police worked the scene and took Luis' body. He'd fallen on a large shard of glass that impaled him and came out his back. "A clear case of him slipping on the wet ground during his," the office paused, "duties." He looked at Jeremy with disgust.

After the police left, Michael warned Jeremy, "You better start explaining."

Jeremy held his hands up, "Ok, ok. Lena told me she had a dream that Renee killed her, and we concocted the story of Renee predicting her death. Lane's crazy ramblings when she visited him were just an extra bonus."

"And the supposed Renee sighting at Nicole's house?" Michael shook him.

"I don't know. That isn't part of the story we agreed to. Lena could have made it up." Jeremy felt the sweat rolling down his back, into his ass crack, and down his legs.

Michael pulled him to the chair and pushed him down, "Tell us everything."

"That's it, I swear. Lena was going to play out her game about Renee and get back at you," he nodded to Nicole, "She hated you. She hated that you're so successful, and she thought she struggled for everything."

"And your stake in all this?" Nicole asked, arms crossed.

Jeremy shrugged, "What can I say? Money, contacts, and a hot piece of ass go a long way in my book."

Jeremy didn't see Nicole's right hook come at him until he was sprawled on the floor. She bent down and grabbed his shirt, "You miserable piece of shit." She pulled her fist back again, and Jeremy flinched.

"Whoa! I think we've all had enough." Michael picked Nicole up as if she weighed nothing and sat her down on the couch. "Stay!" he barked to Jeremy. "We're going to have a talk."

Michael sat down too. "Now, no more bullshit, or I'll have an investigation into you so fast, your head will spin."
Jeremy nodded.

Nicole rubbed her temple. "Let me get this

straight. Lena's story about Renee was bullshit. But Lane really told her he'd been visited by Renee, and he was going to die from hanging, and he ended up dead by his own tshirt."

Jeremy nodded again.

"Your lackey broke my window, which you will pay for, and he used a bottle of perfume to imitate my sister?"

"Hey, the panther piss was part of my game, but I did not have anything to do with the reenactment of your parents' deaths. And I had nothing at all to do with that voice of Lane."

Nicole looked at Jeremy, "So, all bullshit aside, can you tell us anything about what's going on? Because the way I see it, the last things that happened were not residual, and neither were these. How could they if Renee is still alive?"

Jeremy shrugged, "It is like I told you when she came to my house. The construction can dredge things up, and organic things like wood and rock hold vibrations of the past."

"Yes, but it doesn't dredge up live people. And I haven't started construction yet."

"Lane could have wanted to warn you, or perhaps something you've done personally has started the spirits."

"Again," Nicole said, "How can he warn me about something that can't happen. Renee is in a hospital." She thought, "I think. Michael, can you check. Like now?"

"All I can do right now is see if there have been any missing patients. I would have thought if there were, I would have heard. Let me make a call or two."

Nicole turned to Jeremy, "How do we know you aren't bullshitting us?"

"Hey, look, it's true I have a gimmick to get people to buy-in. What they choose to believe is on them."

"Except that we're seeing things that aren't dead." Nicole reminded him.

Jeremy nodded, "Yes, except for that."

Michael returned, "No missing patients." He signed, "I don't fully understand everything I've seen tonight, but we need to figure it out. Fast." Michael glared at Jeremy, "And since you are all we have, you'll help, or I will shut you down."

TWENTY-EIGHT

Renee and Jeremy were hot and sticky on the hay. They were naked and wrapped in each other's arms. They had just taken a sex flight across time and space, and they were enjoying their return to earth.

"That farmer isn't going to be happy seeing all this hay out of his bales." Jeremy commented.

"That's ok. That old man hardly ever comes over to get any. And who is to say what gets in here and digs around. It is a barn. And we are in the country." Renee brushed his worry away.

"I don't need to give your parents another reason to dislike me."

"They dislike everyone. How far can we go with these flights?"

Jeremy shrugged. "I have been flying for a long time. Lately, I've been trying to manipulate things during the flights."

"What do you mean?"

"Like setting things up for myself."

"For example?" she pressed.

Jeremy looked at her, "Do you think I'd be

passing English if I didn't have early knowledge of tests and assignments?"

Renee raised herself up on her arms, about to ask for more details. It sounded useful to her. She could use that for her chemistry class.

"Do you mean going into the future?"

"No, I haven't found a way to do that. But you can use what is currently available. Like in my case, the prepared tests I found."

Suddenly, the pair realized they weren't alone. Renee put her finger to her lips. Slowly and carefully, she peeked out over the top row of hay.

Her father was in the barn with a girl. What the hell, Renee thought. She continued to watch.

"I don't want to do it in the hay. My hair will get all messed up." She heard the girl say.

Renee's heart skipped a beat. She couldn't believe what she was seeing.

"We don't have to do it there. Bend over and pull up your skirt."

The girl turned around, and Renee clapped her hand over her own mouth. It was Lena!

Renee watched, horrified as her father dropped to his knees and began eating Lena out. Lena grabbed onto a supporting post and spread her legs, sticking her rounded ass up as her father moaned and slurped between her legs.

"Oh, you fucking bitch, tell me what you want."

"I want your hard cock, daddy. Please give it to me. I need it."

Renee felt a little sick.

Jeremy belly crawled over to her. Renee put a finger to her lips again and watched his expression as he watched the tableau unfold. He was as shocked and deeply fascinated. Lena was hot, and to see her lay it all out there, he felt his cock get hard.

Her father had pulled his cock out of his zippered shorts, "Come suck your daddy's prick." he waved it at her face as she bent to suck it. "Mmmm. that's it. Take it all in."

The pair watched Lena suck the cock all the way into her mouth, choking slightly. Renee's father pumped it in and out of her mouth, punctuating each suck with a grunt. Finally, he turned Lena around and started fucking her wet pussy. "Oh, yeah, Lena, you're daddy's little cock sucker, aren't you."

Lena moaned, holding on to the post. Her

breasts were pulled out over her tank top and bounced with each thrust. "Oh, daddy, yes. I love it, daddy."

"You love to please me, don't you?"

"Yes, you are my everything."

Renee heard her father grunt and whip Lena around as he pushed her to her knees and exploded over her face. He spent a minute running his penis over her face, and she opened it to take him into her mouth.

"That's it, suck it all off." He reached up to the shelf above them and pulled down some wet wipes. He handed Lena one and said, "Just remember, we have to keep this to ourselves so we can enjoy times like this without anyone knowing."

Lena finished cleaning her face and gave him the wipe. He stuffed it in a plastic bag he produced from his pocket. He pulled a wad of bills from his pocket. "For your school fees."

Lena was back on her feet, standing in front of him. She took the bills and stuffed them in her shirt.

"Let's get you back to your car." He kissed her and then said, "Oh, you missed a spot." He gathered his cum onto his finger from her temple and offered it to Lena, who dutifully licked it off. He stroked her cheeks, "You are so special to me. No one could ever take your place."

Renee was stunned. That is what he used to say to her.

TWENTY-NINE

After the police and Jeremy left, Michael refused to leave Nicole.

"I am a big girl. I am sure I will be fine."

"We could go to my house."

Nicole looked skeptical.

"I think we could both use a break from this house."

Nicole nodded slowly. They drove the short way to Michael's house. The old white farmhouse stood stark in contrast with the riot of leaves on the trees around the house.

"Come on in," he invited.

Nicole stepped into the comfortable home. Much like hers, she suspected he hadn't changed much since his parent's time.

"You know, I did tell mom about you. She liked you. Didn't like your parents."

"Common theme." Nicole sat down. "Comfy," she said of the couch.

Michael shook his head, "I don't know. I'll admit it was really creepy. Had we not been using your own table and had he not brought anything but himself in, I would have thought he set something up. You know, like back in the 1920s spiritualism events." He paused, "I do want to talk about your sister, though."

"I thought we needed a break? It has been a hell of a few days. This is not how I intended to use my vacation."

"Do you want a drink?"

"Oh hell no. I don't drink regularly, and I think I've had my quota for quite some time. Do you have a diet soda?"

"Cherry, if I remember correctly." Michael grabbed them both the same, and he sat next to her. "Look, I don't get everything that's happened. Lena's stories except Lane were bullshit. And I can get behind ghosts. Lane, absolutely. But why would he say Renee was going to kill you? And I don't understand how she can be part of a residual haunting. I know this is hard for you. I remember when we met after your parent's deaths that we never talked about it. We talked about so many other things and were so preoccupied. I really felt like that pond and me, to some extent, were your solace and refuge."

Nicole nodded. "They were. Why do you want to talk about Renee now? I thought we were taking a break."

"How much contact have you had with her

since she was arrested."

"Dog with a bone! I visited her before she was sent to the hospital, and I have written to her. I struggled because I felt guilty that she was locked up and I wasn't. I know that sounds stupid." She shook her head. "I am still trying to process her accusations against my dad."

"People who have been through traumatic experiences have survivor guilt. But you know none of it was your fault, right?"

"Of course! I came to terms with how shitty my parents were years ago. And I wasn't the one who killed them. I am still puzzled as to how she did it, though. We had the same classes from 10 a.m. to lunch, the same lunch, and the same class after lunch. The only time she was really out of my sight for a significant amount of time was before 10 a.m. and after 2 p.m."

"And I remember many students said she was within the 2 p.m. class, albeit asleep."

"It was a study hall. I thought it was crazy that she had to have a study hall as her last period. It was a shame she couldn't just go home. They couldn't ignore the fact that the gun had her prints, and she had a defensive wound on her arm. My mom had her skin under her nails. I still can't believe it in a way."

Michael looked at her and took a drink, "Neither could I. I went over it a dozen times. The students had no reason to lie. Even the teacher said Renee made a point of saying good afternoon to her as she came in." He paused, taking another drink, "I have had some contact with her. Well, more regarding her."

Nicole was a little surprised and a little annoyed. "Oh, I see. She is some weird science project, and you need me to complete the picture?"

Michael's eyes widened, "Absolutely not! I am just very puzzled as to how she did it. She didn't take the stand, and she never explicitly said she did it, but she let her attorney defend her in a way that implied guilt."

"So, what's your point?"

"My point is that I've been waiting to talk to her. I have some pull being a cop, but without good reason, I can't talk to her while she is under treatment and especially not without going through the proper channels, including her doctor."

"So?"

"So I have checked periodically to make sure that her status is the same. They always report that she has been in the prison hospital. She is allowed no visitors except the regular visits from her doctors and counsel visits, which hasn't happened for some time. She has had no phone calls except to her counsel, which has not happened for some time. They continue to evaluate her, and her doctor makes regular visits. She continues to go to one on one therapy. She has the best of everything in the hospital thanks to the fund you set up."

"I don't see what this-"

"When Lena showed up and given your history and the story of Lane, I did some digging on their history."

"My, my, you have been busy."

"It appears that Lena and Lane were a thing for a while."

Nicole smiled, "It would have bothered me a couple years ago, but not now. It doesn't surprise me. Lane liked to spread it around. In fact, the day before I came home and saw you again, he hit on me when I was on campus. And Lena, well, we all know her fixation with being the center of attention. She is like Veronica Lodge oversexed."

"What did he say?"

"He wanted to get laid. I didn't' go home

with him."

"Could you prove that?"

"Yes." Nicole replied, looking Michael in the eye, "I spent the night elsewhere." Michael raised his eyebrow.

"We've covered this." She gave him a withering look.

"Fair enough." Michael smiled. "But, I haven't told you everything."

"About your women or what you found out about this situation?"

Michael shot her a look, "The situation."

"I thought not."

"While he was dating you, he was doing her. It lasted for a few months after you broke up."

Nicole swallowed and shook her head, "Nope, still doesn't surprise me. It pisses me off. Lena always had it in for me for some reason. Hell, she came onto you. I should have known."

"Still not done."

"No? The hits just keep on coming."

"Obviously, Lane is dead. But I listened to the tipster who called in the information about him."

"Let me guess. Lena?"

"No...it sounded like Renee."

Nicole's eyes flew open. "Renee? What? How would she know?"

Michael nodded, "How indeed. Sometimes people in jail get information about stuff outside. They still run drug empires-"

"You aren't suggesting that Renee has a drug empire."

"No, but the voice sounded like hers. At least from what I remember. Would you remember it? The recording is somewhat garbled."

"Sure I would. I'd listen to it if you want me to. If nothing else than to clear up that it couldn't be Renee."

"I'll get the recording sent up here."

Early the next morning, Nicole was awoken by Michael, who reluctantly drove her home.

"You could stay here," he said. "I'd feel better."

"No, I have to get on the contractor, and Mrs. Tenant is coming. I need to clean stuff up and talk to her about future needs."

He left her, and she returned to her bed. She was absolutely exhausted.

Later that morning, when she awoke,

she heard Mrs. Tenant sweeping downstairs. The television was on to some talk show, and occasionally, Nicole heard humming.

Nicole got up and showered, languidly remembering her early morning sexual excursion with Michael, and she touched herself a tad longer in the shower than what would be considered cleaning.

Utterly at peace, she donned her clothing and hopped light-footed downstairs. As soon as she hit the bottom stair, all traces of the television and humming were gone.   T h e house was silent as the grave, except for the trill of laughter surrounding Nicole.

She stepped into the kitchen. "Whoever you are, this is my house. Mine. And you will abide by my rules, or you will be gotten rid of."

The laughter became more maniacal, and the television turned on, the sound of channels flipping becoming increasingly louder. The dishes in the cabinet rattled, and her favorite cup fell out, shattering on the ground.

Nicole's hair moved as a breeze surrounded her and then flew through the plate glass window, shattering it, and with it, the sound of laughter ceased. The television switched off.

THIRTY

Jeremy fumed all the way home. Michael was an asswipe, and Nicole was way too smart for her own good. He was beginning to see why Lena had an ax to grind with Nicole. He could deal with Nicole in his own way, but dealing with Michael was something else.

He was sure Michael was spending the night with Nicole, and that pissed him off more. Still, he better come up with something that sounds concrete or a reason why not to get them off his back. If he could come up with something sympathetic or to put Nicole at ease, he might have a chance left with her.

He was beginning to regret ever having gotten involved with Renee. True, she was hot, and damn, she was into some kinky shit in and out of bed. And she was adventurous once she got used to the idea of threesomes. He remembered that day in the barn shortly before her parents' deaths. They had already forbidden her to see him, but she was crafty, and they used to fuck in the barn and the field behind the barn without her parents knowing. But what they'd seen that day...

The following day he searched through his books and plotted. Jeremy had a plan and was more determined than ever to bag Nicole and get money from her. Especially since she now had money. He went through some of his occult books, looking for points he could use in her home to allow him assured free access for some time to come.

After planning his strategy to repair the damage Luis created, Jeremy sat down with his Tarot cards. Occasionally, he did a Celtic cross for himself, knowing that it was all subject to interpretation. Still, from time to time, it seems spot on.

Today sweat ran down his face at such a rate that no amount of silk handkerchiefs could staunch the flow. This was definitely not good. Not good at all.

In one of the few times Jeremy felt he needed to look at his trade cards, he read the Celtic Cross for himself using the Major Arcana.

He was frightened at what he saw.

The center card was the wheel of fortune upright. No surprise there. Jeremy wanted answers about his future and fate. The two cards on either side were the axis, showing the heart of the matter were the Devil upright, and Temperance reversed, which indicated addiction and extremes. No shit, Jeremy thought. He knew his life was out of balance.

The other two cards forming the vertical axis showed the Tower upright, and Justice reversed. These showed aspects of Jeremy himself, in this case, an impending disaster, and unfairness and dishonesty. Well, the cards aren't wrong, Jeremy mused.

He even made a staff, which consisted of four cards representing a more direct interpretation of the cards. The Devil, coupled with the Hanged Man upright, indicated a release was in order, which could be good, but when Death related with Temperance, this meant definite decay and stagnation.

Jeremy put the cards together again and shuffled them in impatience. He didn't believe this stuff. He placed the cards again. Devil, Temperance, Tower, Justice, Hanged Man, Death.

Shit, damn, fuck, hell. This just couldn't be. Jeremy grunted and pulled the cards up again.

One more time.

After the third placement gave the same

results, Jeremy shook his head and put the cards away. Looking through his stash of occult communication tools, he chose a vintage Ouija board.

Jeremy decided to dispense with the bells and whistles and just get down to the real heart of the matter. He opened the box on the Crystal Gazer ouija board and put his fingers on the planchette. "I need a spirit who is willing to answer a few questions about recent events for me. If there is a willing spirit, please step forward." Jeremy settled in.

"Who am I speaking to?"

"L-U-I-S"

"Luis, thank you. How did you die?"

"G-L-A-S-S"

"Did you do it to yourself?"

"N-O"

"Who did it?"

"S-O-L-D-I-E-R"

Jeremy remembered the story Lena told him about the ghost she'd come face to face within the house.

"I want to talk about others. Where is Lane Kincaid?"

"D-E-A-D"

"How did he die?"

"H-A-N-G"
"Who killed him?"
"R-E-N-E-E"
Jeremy paused.
"Where is Lena Gammon?"
"D-E-A-D"
"Where is Lena's body?"
"W-A-T-E-R"
"Is Nicole Bichey in danger?"
"Y-E-S"
"Am I in danger?"
"Y-E-S"
"Is Michael Madigan in danger?
"Y-E-S"
"What is Michael in danger of?"
"   D-E-A-T-H"
"What is Nicole in danger of?"
"D-E-A-T-H"
"What am I in danger of?"

Jeremy didn't have to read the letters to know the answer.

With shaky hands, Jeremy dialed Nicole's number.

Outside, it began to snow.

THIRTY-ONE

It was seven p.m. when the short, balding policeman arrived on her doorstep. He was not in his typical uniform but in a flannel shirt and heavy pants. He had on Wellingtons, and a long scarf draped around his neck. Behind him was a snowmobile. It had started to snow again, and the wind was bitterly cold. He said he was Officer John Rutledge.

"Are you related to Sheriff Rutledge?"

"He's my dad."

Nicole nodded, "Your mom and dad took my sister and me in for a few nights when my parents were killed."

Officer Rutledge regarded her for a moment. "I remember that. Hell, I think everyone does. My mom was anxious about you both. Even after they found the gun and your sister's prints."

"Your parents are good people," Nicole asked if he wanted a cup of coffee.

He waved her off. "When did you say she left?"

"She said she was going for a walk four days ago. She was tired of being stuck indoors."

Nicole's voice wavered.

"Why did you wait so long to call?" he asked.

"She showed up unannounced, and she and I aren't exactly friends. We have known each other since high school but fell out. She came back to talk about stuff; I am not her keeper. She left a note." Nicole produced the paper for the cop. "I was also busy trying to ensure we could get out if necessary and trying to keep ahead of the snow. With the note, I assumed she came back and went to spend time with her friend, Jo."

"Who is Jo?"

"I don't know her. Jo de Beauvoir was someone Lena met at the High Tunnel a couple days before she went walking. I think she works at the Qwick Mart in town."

He called in a patrolman to go to the Qwick Mart to talk to Jo. "Yeah? No kidding? Will do." He hung up and faced Nicole, "It would seem Jo de Beauvoir has been A.W.O.L. from her job since Ms. Gammon went on her walk. We're going to have to look around the house to see if there is anything else we can find as a clue to her whereabouts. Do you have her cell phone number?"

A knock was heard at the door. Opening it, Nicole was surprised to see Michael Madigan standing there. He was covered in a fine dusting of snow, and his ears and cheeks were pink. "I heard about the call on my radio. Can I help?"

Nicole was stunned. Officer Rutledge came to her rescue. "Michael, we're going to need help. As you can imagine, we are short-handed for this sort of thing, especially in the middle of another snow event."

Michael came in and stood by the door. "Just tell me what I need to do."

Nicole gave the phone number to the pair and a description of Lena and what she had been wearing. "What can I do?"

Officer Rutledge looked at the number and took a photo of it. Then he dialed it. "Voice mail. Stay here and monitor your phone in case she calls. We can't search in this snow. Oh, we will need something of hers that has her scent. Since she went off walking, that would be the first step. As for Ms. de Beauvoir-"

Michael spoke up, "I checked her side business, and it doesn't seem too legitimate. It seems more like a front for prostitution or at least a sugar daddy situation. I will get the phone company to ping its whereabouts. I can give a description and will ask others if she has any distinguishing marks."

Officer Rutledge nodded, "I'll let the guys know you'll be assisting and that they are to give you cooperation."

"Right. I've already called in and let the post know where I am."

Rutledge turned to Nicole, "We can't get out there tonight, but at first light, we'll be out. I am going to try and see what I can get from pinging Lena's phone. We'll get a search party set up. Generally, we get volunteers when anything big happens, so we will see who shows up tomorrow morning and get it organized. I'll be back around 7:30 a.m."

Officer Rutledge left, and Michael kissed Nicole, "I gotta get to work." he apologized.

"Go get 'em."

About 7:30 a.m. Officer Rutledge arrived with two other officers and six volunteers. The volunteers were predominantly farmers and retired older people who owned snowmobiles and heavy equipment. Their names and contact information were scheduled for follow-up if needed. They were unable to use the K-9 officers they had on hand because one was an air scent dog and the other a tracker. Because of the snow and the volunteers, a K-9 officer could not be effective, but Officer Rutledge took Lena's clothing and bagged it.

Office Rutledge briefed the group, "We have two missing women. Lena Gammon, who some of you may remember when she was younger, was seen walking away from this house in this direction." he gestured towards his back. "We can't get through via calling, but her phone was pinged back in that direction."

Michael chimed in, "The other woman, Jo de Beauvoir, is also local. We don't know that they are together, but they were known to have a casual intimate relationship. Additionally, Jo didn't answer my text, and a call to her went to voicemail. Her phone pinged in the same area as Lena's."

They split the group into three groups: two snowmobiles that scouted ahead and two groups on foot. They kept in contact via a group text. Most of the on-foot team members had snowshoes, and they made good progress to the back of the property where the pings were located.

The snowmobile team did not find

anything amiss throughout the first open area they checked, which could have been because of the fresh snow. The foot teams followed the ping information for both phones. They were within 75 meters of each other.

The two groups saw the barn located on the Gutzwiller's property. One group headed to the barn and the other kept outside working an arms-length apart, looking for any signs of disturbance or clues.

Shortly after the team entered the barn, they texted the group and told them they'd found what they believed was Jo. There was evidence that she was murdered. Her phone was nearby.

Immediately the volunteers were removed, and the police blocked the barn. While the local authorities worked on the crime scene, Michael and the volunteers went back to the house.

Nicole offered everyone tea, coffee, warm soup, and sandwiches while they waited for additional instructions. Meanwhile, Michael called and asked for an update on the request for phone records. He walked back down to talk to Rutledge, "Well, there are several calls between Jo and Lena and some spicy texts indicating the intimate nature of their relationship."

Rutledge looked at Michael, "What is your skin in this game. How do you know all these folks?"

"I was a few years ahead of Lena and Nicole. The other night we were at the High Tunnel. Jo and Lena hit on me, and when it didn't work, they worked the room and apparently each other. It shows a short call to Jo from Lena the day they both disappeared. It matches up with the time frame Nicole said Lena left."

"You and Nicole a thing?"

Michael smiled slightly, "I'd like to think so."

"Then you have to be off the case."

"What do you mean?"

"She wasn't exactly friends with either girl and one was killed on a property that recently transferred to her. Until she has an alibi, she is a suspect."

Michael's training told him Rutledge was right, but it rankled him. He had no doubt Nicole was innocent. Michael thought of Lena's game in the back of his mind and how the endgame turned out for her. But he couldn't tell Rutledge that. He'd laugh him right back to the house.

Instead, Michael nodded, "Understood. It will be interesting what else you get off that phone. There are several texts from people you're going to want to follow up with. I'll send you the information. If at any time you feel it is appropriate, I'm glad to help."

Rutledge shook Michael's hand. "Don't get too comfortable. You're a suspect, too. You're going to have to provide us an alibi." Rutledge pulled one of the cops over. "Take him back to the house and take his statement. Send the volunteers home. Until we secure what we need from here, we can't do any more searching."

It was nearly three o'clock in the afternoon when Rutledge told Nicole they were taking a pickup with a blade back to remove the evidence and the body. The same officer who took Michael's statement took hers. Michael was on duty, and Nicole told them she was at Jeremy's house. The pickup would serve as the coroner's vehicle to deliver Jo to the coroner in Marion for autopsy.

The day had taken a toll on everyone. Despite her suspect status, the search team lingered over Nicole's buffet. Nicole was numb with shock. She was on autopilot as she refilled cups. She felt so sad for a woman she hardly knew, and she felt so badly about the conversation Lena started about Jo.

Lena was not a good person. She was mean and spiteful, but Nicole couldn't help but think now that perhaps some of Lena's story was true.

In the middle of the night, Nicole heard a knock on the door. Who could that be in this weather, she wondered.

"Nicole, I thought you might like some company." Michael stood shivering at the door.

"Oh, Michael, now isn't the time for a booty call." Nicole started to close the door.

He stopped her. "I am not here for that. I am here just to make sure you are ok."

Nicole stared at him. "I'm fine."

"You don't look it. How about me coming in and fixing you tea. We can talk, or you can sleep."

Nicole looked skeptical.

Michael held his hands up. "You can kick me out at any time."

Reluctantly, Nicole opened the door, "Come in, but don't be an idiot."

"I would never dream of it."

Nicole pulled the tea out.

"That's a lot of tea."

"I love tea. Black tea is my favorite, but I love chamomile, hibiscus, all sorts of English and Irish breakfast teas. And, of course, Turkish. I read the leaves."

Michael smiled, "Maybe you'll read them for me sometime. But for now, chamomile with a little citrus in it." He grated a little orange zest into her teapot. When it was ready, he strained it into her cup.

"Mmmm. How do you know so much about tea?" It was good.

Michael shrugged. "You aren't the only one who loves tea."

As Michael drank the warm liquid, she was fascinated with his Adam's apple bobbing up and down. She looked up to his jawline marred with stubble and to his glistening lips.

"You, you don't think I had anything to do with-" she asked.

"Not for one minute." Michael quickly said without missing a beat. "You think I had-"

"Not for one minute."

Nicole curled up with Michael on the couch. They settled into a comfortable silence.

THIRTY-TWO

Nicole awoke to the smell of crisp bacon and buttery toast. She stretched on the couch and was disappointed to find Michael, not with her. She looked briefly at her phone. A text from Jeremy confirmed he had spoken with the cops and confirmed her story. Smiling, she put the phone down as Michael came into the living room.

"Good morning," he smiled at her, "I called in today and decided to fix you breakfast. I just need to plate it."

"Could I get a hug first?"

"Could be really dangerous." he smiled.

"I hope so," she replied, holding her arms out to him. Planting a warm kiss on his lips, she could feel herself go liquid. She leaned back on the couch and pulled his already turgid cock out. "I hope you're ready to settle in for a while." she smiled.

Later that morning, Michael and Nicole spent time removing snow. About six inches dropped overnight, and it was frigid outside.

"Thank you so much. I don't feel so isolated.

My bike is useless, but I still have my parent's cars if I really need to leave. "Nicole grabbed the shovel she used. "Hey, where's the other? It here when I was shoveling a few days ago."

Michael looked around, "I don't know." He looked into the garage, "There it is. You must have put it away."

Nicole's cell phone rang.

"It's Jeremy." Nicole mouthed to Michael. She put it on speaker. "What do you have for us?"

Jeremy spoke. He sounded out of breath and scared, "I don't have a lot of time. I did a Ouija board session. Lena is dead, Lane is dead, we are in danger. I think I know what is going on. I taught Renee how to astral project, and I think she -" Jeremy started to break up.

"Jeremy? Jeremy?"

"-you can manipulate the material world.-"

"Jeremy? You aren't making sense."

"Flights manipulate the living-"

"Jeremy?"

The phone went dead.

Nicole looked at her battery, "Empty. That's odd. It was full a few minutes ago."

"What's his number?" Michael said.

"Let me plug this in. We'll have to look it up

online."

Michael looked it up while Nicole plugged in her phone. He dialed Jeremy's number. "Huh, no answer. I'll leave a message."

THIRTY-THREE

Shit, fire, hell, and damnation! All I wanted was some contacts, some pussy, and money. Jeremy sighed. Night flights when his victims were asleep were all well and good to set things up to supplement his income, but it was becoming harder to keep up the facade. It was a very complex web, and trying to keep things straight was difficult, even if he did try to pass it off as seeing the future.

He tried to call Nicole back, but her phone went to voicemail. Another call came in after, but when he picked it up, no one answered.

He was going to take another flight. From the time he was in high school, he enjoyed astral projection. He read everything he could, studied techniques, and practiced. It took him some time, but once he got it, he was hooked.

Jeremy took flight whenever he didn't want to deal with reality. When he started dating Renee, their relationship was tight. She was fun and a great lay. He remembered the day that he showed her how to fly and manipulate the world around them while in flight. She was a quick learner. That was the day they saw

Lena and Renee's father together.

He told Renee during one of their many flights, "During astral projection, your spiritual body disconnected from your physical being but is kept connected through a silver cord. Your life goes forward on the primal stage or earthly plane as usual. Your spiritual body travels and encounters others on the astral plane. If the cord was cut, you would die. But," he paused dramatically, "But if the cord is kept intact, you could fly astrally as long as you like.

Jeremy found that while most practitioners agreed no technique could manipulate the primal stage during astral travels, he could. All you had to do was focus on the aura colors surrounding whatever you wanted to manipulate wherever you wanted to be in the present, and you could interact with the living.

He'd once read about a hospital mental patient, Alexander Ferguson, yet the hospital administration kept getting complaints about the man. They asked that the hospital come back to his hometown and take him back to the hospital. The hospital superintendent, Dr. John Athon, kept writing that the man was still in the hospital.

One   particularly   brutal   recounting

involved the patient in his hometown and beating a man to a pulp. After hearing of the event, the superintendent went to the patient to talk with him.

What Ferguson told Dr. Athon was astounding. He mentioned times, places, dates, where he had been, and what he did. They all corresponded with the complaints the hospital received.

When Dr. Athon asked how he did it, Ferguson smiled and told a tale of his "flying visit. "I didn't see anybody on the road. I was so high up. I came with the pigeons; they were a'cheering me. Ha, ha! I didn't make no time at all. The colors were so bright, I could touch everything through their colors. I got home first. I am going back tomorrow. The whisky made my head swim and run against the lightning, which singed my whiskers and colored 'em red." It was suggested by an author who studied the patient's case that his mental illness made it easier for him to vacate his body.

That is when Jeremy began studying auras and conducted his own aura color touching experiments. Tonight, he was going on another. Jeremy wanted to see where Renee was and wanted to check on Nicole. He could hardly believe he was starting to give a damn about something else other than money and pussy.

He lay on his bed and turned on the thunderstorm track. Regressing himself into the astral plane, he drifted toward Nicole's house. It was such a silent night. As he passed over the pond near her home, he saw something unusual. He could see the pond's vague indent in the snow and a distinct hole at the edge of the pond. He zoomed down to take a closer look and entered the hole. He screamed as he came face to face with Lena, her eyes open and gazing at the ice above her.

Jeremy left the water, feeling his astral body pulsing. He saw the barn near the pond with a light on. Moving inside, Jeremy saw a woman's body slumped on its side, head on the ground and her ass in the air. Looking closer, he could see her mutilated insides spilling out of the place where her pussy should be.

Jeremy felt so sick. He ordinarily felt safe and invincible in the astral world; he suddenly had a feeling of dread and a sense nothing would ever be the same.

"It's time for you to fly. For good." He heard a familiar voice say, "You deserve this."

Jeremy saw the flash of the knife strike his chest as he watched his silver cord curl downward and dissipate.

THIRTY-FOUR

Despite the new snow, the police returned to search again with a cadaver dog. Paolo was a labrador-golden retriever mix on loan from the State Police. The police took him outside. "It's good with a bit of wind. If there are remains, it will be easier for him to hit on the scent.

At first, the dog hit on the barn. His trainer redirected him and began to hit further away. Shortly after 2:30 p.m. Officer Rutledge appeared and told Nicole and Michael that they found Lena frozen in the cattle pond on the Gutzwiller's property.

They brought a diver in and had him pull Lena's body from the water. They cordoned off the area. A storm was coming in, and barring something the weather wouldn't destroy, the evidence was little and would have to be collected later.

After he left, Nicole thought a nap was what she needed. She would lay down for a few minutes before she started dinner. On the news, they showed most of the roads covered in snow, and they were asking for help from as far away as Texas.

So tired. The week had been so stressful—Lena. What a horrible way to die. Did you scream for help, and I didn't hear you? How hard did you struggle to get out?

Instead of sleeping, Nicole found herself wandering around the house in a circle. The sitting room, living room. Laundry and kitchen. She found herself at the front of the house, looking at the narrow stairway.

Nicole could see the short wooden attic door was partially open in the dim light coming from her attic room. Nicole felt a breeze come down the stairs and saw the door sway lightly. Was that a shadow she saw crossing in front of the door?

Sinking to her knees to get a better look, Nicole smiled. It was her imagination, she was sure. Overtiredness, that's what it was. It was the overtiredness that made her think that someone was in the house.

A nice cup of hot chocolate and some brownies were just the things. After filling the tea kettle, Nicole baked some brownies she made from a mix. Despite her comfort food and drink, Nicole was on edge.

She flipped on the television and heard that rain and freezing rain were in store. Flooding was expected in the morning. *At least everyone will be able to carry on,* Nicole thought.

Turning the furnace up a notch, Nicole rubbed her arms. For the temperature change outside, it sure didn't feel warmer inside! The melting snow silhouetted against the dark sky, and a full moon shed its light over the silent countryside. The bare, ice-covered branches gleamed in the moonlight, giving an eerie glow to the landscape.

Remembering Jeremy's call, she tried to reach him. No answer. Nicole sat down on the living room couch and started researching astral projection online. It seemed to be a variation of spacing out or daydreaming only with your eyes closed. *I have got to be crazy,* she thought as she settled down in the living room to try it.

She closed her eyes.

Concentrating on moving into the clouds above herself, Nicole felt herself relax. Floating, floating, Nicole began to feel herself leaving her body. For her, it was so odd to see her body as she floated ever upward. She could see her body, a slender silver cord between her astral and human bodies. Drifting, skimming the edges of the room. Before she could really enjoy the new experience, Nicole heard a knock at the door.

Opening the door from her astral body, Nicole peered into the darkness. A figure stepped from the shadows.

"Hi!" chirped the figure with a wave. "What's up?" Hazel eyes sparkled mischievously from under the brim of a white plastic rain hat.

Nicole stared, confused. "Who are you?" she asked.

The figure stepped in, not waiting for an invitation. Rain dripped down the white slicker, and a tangled mass of red curls waved starkly across her shoulders. "What kind of greeting is that?" As the figure breezed in, Nicole could see a silver cord attached to her.

"Renee!"

"God, it's been a while!" she breathed, pulling off her slicker and hat. Renee was wearing a seafoam green cable knit sweater and slim-fitting button-fly Levis. The woman plopped down on the couch and propped her feet up on the oak coffee table. "Got anything to eat?"

Nicole could only stare. "But how?"

"Good. You remember me. You've learned how to astral project. Congratulations." She leaned back and stretched her arms out. "Could I at least beg a drink? The path here wasn't exactly in the best condition."

Nicole signed. "Fine, Renee. Tea? Coffee? Something stronger?"

"Bacardi cola, if you please."

She poured the drink. "Renee, if you've escaped, you need to go back, or you'll never get out."

Laughter rang throughout the house. "Don't you get it? We are astral projecting. I don't have to get out. I can do whatever I want, regardless of being locked up. I am the sun and the moon. I am the stars. I am your favorite fantasy, and I am your worst nightmare. I am hope and despair in one impossibly beautiful and hateful package. That's who I am. "

"You're talking nonsense."

"Oh, no, not at all," she said dismissively. "Jo was good," the red-haired visitor commented, rolling her eyes upward.

"I don't know what you mean," denied Nicole.

"No good, Nicole. I heard your conversation with Lena. Tsk tsk. Jo would have enjoyed it more if she wasn't tied to the barn support."

"You killed her!" But why? How? You have

been in hospital for..."

"For years. Time is irrelevant for me." Renee replied coolly. "A glorious flight. Just like with parents. How do you think I was in school and killing them at the same time."

Nicole went verbally after her, "I felt sorry for you. I understood why you would do that to our parents. But why the others."

THIRTY-FIVE

When Lena received Jo's text, she couldn't have been happier—getting away from Nicole and getting laid? She met Jo at the Gutzwiller's barn and soon found herself riding Jo's mouth. The girl's eyes were closed, and both women were moaning in pleasure.

Lena couldn't help herself, mashing her crotch on Jo's face and urging her to use her tongue faster. The figure looked on, enraged. *Bitches.*

Soon, Lena was crying out in pleasure, soaking Jo's face in cum. They switched places, the watcher noted, and both of them were eating each other out, rutting in the mud like swine.

Jo never had it so good from anyone. Lena had texted her and asked her to meet her at the barn. She got a ride out to the property as her car was being worked on. From there, Jo walked the short way to the barn through the snow.

Lena has been spectacular the night they left the bar. She'd even talked about helping her find a better job. Jo would have been happier if Lena had come to her apartment. But she had been adamant that they meet in the barn. And who was Jo to question the kink when she was guaranteed a good time? Besides, it was a small price to pay for a possible job in a software firm.

A cloud of warm air enveloped the pair as their breathing became labored, and their voice rose in saucy sonance.

"When I got your text, I didn't realize you were into the rustic thing." Jo laughed.

"Huh? You texted me!"

They had no time to discuss it further.

Suddenly, Jo looked up. With the agility and speed of a cat, she tied Jo's arms to a post.

"H-hey, what's going on?" Jo said nervously.

Lena's eyes narrowed at the intruder. "What the hell do you want?"

"So very much." The interloper snapped Lena's hands in cuffs, locked the door, and slowly smiled, the emotion not quite reaching her eyes, "But I am sure you'll gladly give it."

Like lightning, the watcher moved behind Lena and pulled her ratted hair.

"Spread your legs." The intruder ordered Jo. "Get down there," she forced Lena to her knees.

"Why are you here? If you want to join in, just say so." Jo whimpered. "We can all have fun," she pleaded.

"Lick that pussy, Lena, like your life depends on it!"

Despite the situation, Jo and Lena lost themselves in the moment as their captor issued commands. But it seemed the person was a voyeur and if it allowed her to get off and them to get out, an unspoken "so be it" lay between Jo and Lena.

Finally, after Jo and Lena had shuddered to orgasm several times, the watcher grabbed Jo by her hair and hauled her to her knees, pushing Lena on her back.

Lena cried out as her back scraped the dirt and debris of the old barn. Jo sobbed quietly, as her position was difficult with her arms tied at an awkward angle. Their captor commanded Jo to lay on top of Lena and eat her pussy while their nemesis thrust a dildo in Jo from behind.

Lena closed her eyes as Jo's dark head went down between her brown thighs and once again began to arouse her. Lena laid back, opening her legs wider as she saw their captor insert her big dildo inside Jo's shaved lips.

The pleasure started to work against the pain. Jo began to twitch and moan, pushing her slender hips back to meet the thrusts of the plastic phallus. She moaned even louder and thrust her tongue into Lena's pink pussy as the dildo moved to her ass.

It was *too* intense. Almost painful. It was painful. Jo lifted her face and turned to see their captor thrust something inside her. And the pain was so deep, so intense. Jo cried out, "Please, no! Please stop!"

Lena saw the knife flying in and out of Jo's already dying, bleeding body. Jo was gasping, blood spurting out of her mouth, "Now I lay me down to sleep…" she burbled.

Blood spatter washed over Lena's body, and she felt Jo's life leave her. Jo's last bowel movement splashed over her face and chest, mixing in the blood and bits of viscera.

The torturer looked at Lena and laughed. The expression changed the anger in an instant, and the figure stalked toward Lena.

Whimpering, Lena remembered her childhood and how she ran wild, much to the chagrin of her elderly parents, who had had Lena and her sister, Jackie, much later in life.

Lena remembered the soldier in the Bichey house and the drive back to her own home. She thought back to the kiss Renee's father gave her that night after Jackie left the car, which sparked their relationship and changed her life forever. All the other lovers, school, and Jo bolted through her mind.

Lena felt her bowels vacate.

THIRTY-SIX

Renee continued to sip her drink. "I've come to put you out of your wretched misery." As the words were spoken, Nicole heard the clink of metal. Whirling, she saw the woman holding a butcher's knife.

Sobered by her words, Nicole observed the other woman. There was a wild recklessness in her eyes that was somehow more dangerous than the knife she held. Nicole took quick stock of her options. She could make it out the back door. But where would she go? There was no one for over a mile, and the snow and ice would make it impossible. And she didn't know Renee's abilities.

Finally, Nicole decided to go for it. "You'd better get the hell out of my house. Now. You obviously were able to make it here. You can obviously find your way back to wherever." Nicole turned to go to the front door.

"It's no good. You wouldn't get very far," Renee sneered, twirling the knife on her fingertip. "I'm going to enjoy this." The woman held up her finger. Blood was sliding in a single ruby red stream down her finger. Raising it to her lips, Renee smiled, "Delicious."

Nicole suppressed a shudder and instead shrugged. "Maybe I would; maybe I wouldn't," Nicole said cautiously. "But don't you think it's only fair that you tell me why?"

"Isn't it plain? You didn't confront Lena, who was fucking your boyfriend, so I took care of it. Jo wanted Michael, Lena wanted them both, so I took that out of your life too. Our parents treated us like shit. I took care of that too."

"And Luis, too? What was his crime?"

"Oh no, that was the soldier. Not me." Renee laughed. "I believe Corporal Wolverton's exact words were, 'Bastard Mexicans.'"

Renee slammed her glass down on the table, shattering it and sending tiny piercing shards of glass all over Nicole and the room. "Why couldn't you ever stand up to anyone? You are just like mom. She didn't stand up to our father when he used me, and I am sure she knew about him and Lena fucking like dogs in the barn on the regular. You had to know things weren't right between you and Lane, and yet, you couldn't stand up for yourself. No! Because you are weak! Just-like-our-parents."

Nicole felt her mouth go dry and her

underarms go wet with sweat. She could feel the adrenaline pouring through her body in waves causing her to feel dizzy but very alert.

Looking down, Renee rubbed the blood she saw on her hand all over her face and started laughing. Her cachinnation ratcheted higher and higher until she sounded like a banshee keening for a loss.

"I didn't know any of this. Dad never touched me. I am so sorry for you."

"Of course not. Dad already had enough of mom, and he knew you would talk," Renee reasoned practically. "What did he need you or me for when he had his slut, Lena?" Her eyes clouded, "He told me I was special." In an instant, her eyes beamed a hateful glare, "I don't need your pity."

Nicole was silent, and her mind was reeling. Her family was so much more fucked up than she knew. Nicole tried to buy time. "How did you kill Jo and Lena so easily?"

The woman made a face as if they were conspirators in a childish prank. "Easy when you use aura colors around things for strength, like you did to pour a drink, wield a knife, or shoot a gun. I waited for Jo to show up, and then I went in. I let them play with each other to get them off guard. That is the key. I tied her up and took care of Jo first. Lena realized it was me after I told her I saw her fuck dad in the barn for school fees."

Renee paused, savoring the memory, "Lena was a bit of a disappointment. She was far too easy, but then, that was Lena." She snorted. "It was so easy to throw her in the pond. No one around." Renee stabbed the knife in Nicole's direction, "In the many days I spent in my room, mom left me with my books. Astral projection. And Jeremy taught me how to fly and manipulate the world around me."

"Why didn't you just manipulate people and get out of the hospital?"

"It's not that easy." Renee replied, her voice tinged with regret.

"You don't really think you are going to get away with all of this, do you?"

Renee shrugged negligently. "Doesn't matter. The mistake I made with mom and dad was believing imprints of you don't stay with the dead. Including fingerprints. I fixed that this time. They think I am still in the crazy hospital. You have an alibi. And even if they don't believe it, I won't be around to be caught." Renee lunged for Nicole.

THIRTY-SEVEN

As Renee came for Nicole, Nicole crashed back into her body, her concentration broken. Her reentry felt like an awful airplane landing with much turbulence. She landed with a thud and inhaled deeply.

Renee laughed at Nicole's abrupt transition. Seeing a temporary reprieve, Nicole seized the opportunity and ran out of the house, slipping on the icy snow. Her knees scraped the ground. Nicole suddenly felt so tired of trying. All good things must come to an end. Isn't that what Mom always said somewhat sadly after Nicole's slumber party guests would go home? Nicole could hear Renee cursing behind her and above her. She scrambled on her bloodied knees to get farther away.

Renee pulled Nicole's long, red hair savagely from her face. "Where do you think you're going? You owe me."

Nicole bit back a cry. She could feel handfuls of hair pulled from her scalp, and tears pricked her eyelids. "You did everything on your own, for you. It was all revenge on those who wronged you. I wronged you in your mind because I wasn't good enough, like everyone else. I owe you nothing."

"You will beg me to kill you before you're through. If you thought Jo's death was painful, just wait." With that, Renee stuffed Nicole into a deep hole with snow walls.

"See if you can crawl your way out of that one, cunt. Everything is frozen again, and as you can see," Renee laughed, "It's snowing again. And they will think you killed yourself." Renee turned to walk away.

"You've miscalculated again, Renee." Nicole taunted.

Renee whirled around and narrowed her eyes. "How so?"

It was Nicole's time to laugh. She continued laughing, her eyes closed. This was not how she was going to die. Not today. And Renee was not going to get the best of her anymore. Renee was yelling at her, but Nicole was no longer listening. She was concentrating, trying to send herself back to her body. Concentrating, Nicole felt herself rise above her sister. She drifted toward the house. If she could get to her phone!

A pair of headlights zoomed up her driveway, flinging snow.

Michael! Nicole didn't want him in this.

"Nicole, get back down here, or I will kill him now." Renee was enraged, her voice jagged with venom.

Nicole could see Michael get out of the car and run to the house.

"Nicole, wake up! Nicole!" he called her.

"Don't you do it, Nicole. Don't leave, or I will kill him."

Nicole ignored Renee and pushed herself to fly back. The silver cord began to thicken as she came closer to her body.

This time she was prepared, and it was much more fluid. As her astral body rejoined her physical body, Nicole opened her eyes. She turned to Michael, "Renee is here. You have to get out. She will kill you." Nicole stood up.

"No, I know how to stop it. Jeremy wrote a note. If we wound Renee here, she has to go back. Or she will die if it is bad enough. Either way that will give us time for our next move."

Renee burst through the door, knife in hand. Her silver cord pulsed strongly. She slashed wildly at Michael, catching his forearm. He yelped and held a hand to it, backing out of her reach.

"You won't make it out of here," she spat

at Michael.

"You mean you won't. We know how it works." Nicole warns.

"Neither of you has power over me." Renee cackled.

Nicole drew closer to Renee. "Then do it. Kill me."

"Die!" Renee bellowed, lunging for Nicole.

As Renee made her move, Michael reached out and pushed her. The knife fell, spinning by its handle on the floor. Nicole stuck her foot out and tripped Renee.

Renee stumbled. Her cry fairly shook the house. Knick-nacks fell from the shelves, and Nicole could hear the dishes crashing in the kitchen. Michael and Nicole stood motionless as a bright light filled the room. They saw Renee collapse on the floor, bright red blood seeping out from under her body. Her shimmering slender cord dimmed.

Behind the light, a dark, fiercer presence stepped forward. "She is not for me," it said fading into the shadows.

Renee disappeared.

EPILOGUE

"I feel sorry for Nicole and Michael," Jo said sadly.

"What about me?" Lena complained.

"Jesus, Lena, can't you ever think about anyone other than yourself?" Lane took a jab at the whining woman.

"I told you that you were going to die." Lindsey gloated.

"Asshole," Lena spoke to Lindsey, "You paid to fuck me."

"You were legal and I wasn't the only one to pay you. At least I warned you about your death. Not my fault you didn't figure it out." Lindsey grinned, "Want to fuck now? You've never had sex as a ghost."

Lena contemplated the idea, but said nothing.

"What happened to that little prick, Jeremy?" Dee asked.

"Such language from the pious virgin! Since when did you care about anyone other than yourself?" Lindsey goaded his wife.

Dee hit Lindsey with a cast iron frying pan, slightly denting his skull.

"He lived," Jo supplied. "Too bad, I would have liked a go at him."

Lane looked at Jo, "You can have a go with me."

Jo giggled.

"What are all of you complaining about? In my immediate proximity, I am stuck with two whores, two people that sum up the stench of the human race, and numerous others that roll through." Corporal Wolverton, the soldier veteran, lamented, "Bastard Mexicans."

"*¡Vete a la mierda!* Fuck you!" Luis smacked the soldier in the head with his glass piece, leaving a bloodless line on his forehead.

"How dare you talk about others when you killed me?" Luis brightened, "At least I know all languages now."

Nicole half turned her head and hissed, "Could all of you shut the fuck up? Or I swear to god, I will cleanse you the fuck off the face of this earth."

She turned back to Michael and held his hand. After Renee and the dark *thing* disappeared, Nicole called the police. It took some time, and Nicole was terrified during her wait. She was petrified Michael would die.

The ambulance transported them to

Marion General Hospital. Nicole was justifiably distraught and had few superficial cuts and a strained ankle.

Michael was different. The knife cut him deeply, nicking the radial artery. The surgeon repaired the damage, and now Michael lay sedated in the bed.

Nicole ran her lips over his hand. So close. They were so close.

"Ms. Bichey?"

Nicole, nerves raw, turned sharply and stood defensively. Behind her was a police officer. "Yes?"

The police officer spoke, removing his hat. "I'm Officer Masteam. I work with Officer Madigan," he gestured to the figure in the bed. Masteam fingered the brim of his hat, "I, uh, I wanted to take your statement."

Nicole told him the story she'd concocted with more detail as she waited with Michael. She was at home when an unknown intruder came in. Nicole heard the intruder rummaging around and came down from her room to investigate. It was then that he attacked her. She ran outside, and the intruder followed. When she saw Michael showed up, the burglar attacked Michael, too. She couldn't give a description as it was dark and she was too busy trying to stay alive.

Officer Masteam took Nicole's information and thanked her. "We still have some investigation, but we believe whoever came into your house may have killed Jo and Lena. The knife didn't have prints. The only prints we found in the barn belonged to the two murdered women. We believe the person killed Jo and then dragged Lena to the lake and slipped her under the ice." He shivered, "Bad way to die. Then whoever it was circled back after you, hoping to trap and kill you."

Nicole nodded. What else could she say?

Officer Masteam cleared his throat and continued. He looked intently at Nicole, "I have a second reason for being here. We can't tell you everything, but we thought you would want to know, your sister will survive. She somehow cut herself in the chest. It wasn't enough to kill."

Nicole stared at him.

Officer Masteam gestured to Michael, "Tell him we're all behind him. He's been a great detective in training." He grew thoughtful, "He was so fascinated by your sister's case. He wanted to keep track of her. I don't think he quite believed she killed your parents." He put his hat back on and tipped the brim at Nicole, "Well, I will let you get back to it."

Nicole thanked him and turned back to Michael.

Michael's eyes flew open. "She's still here!"

Continued in
All is Calm.
Coming in Summer 2022

Author's Note

I rearranged some time and space for this book. The following are real locations, institutions, and businesses:

- Indiana State Police
- Indiana State University (Terre Haute, Indiana)
- Indiana University (Bloomington, Indiana)
- St. Mary of the Wood College (Terre Haute, Indiana)
- Taylor University (Upland, Indiana)
- Ivanhoe's (Upland, Indiana): a wonderful family restaurant with the absolute best ice cream treat selection,burgers and hot dogs in Indiana.
- Art's Pizza (Anderson, Indiana, not Upland) is home of the my favorite pizza. I have been eating Art's "Around the World" pizza for over 47 years.
-

The High Tunnel Tavern is based (in part) on the history of Upland, but it does not exist, much to the disappointment of Michael, my husband.

The patient who astral projected and who

is mentioned in this book, is real. This is a documented case from Central State Hospital and quoted in "Doubles: The Enigma of the Second Self" by Rodney Davies.

I wish to thank the following people:

- Michael Kobrowski, for his unwavering support. Even when my writing makes him scared of me.
- Jennifer Williams, MS, LMHC, for her mental health expertise. Sorry/not sorry, for scaring you.
- Jose Beyer, for his language assistance. *¡Muchísimas gracias!*
- My test readers, you are the best!

My music muses were: Foreigner "Agent Provocateur", Foreigner "Four", GTR, Joel Hoekstra "13", The Left Banke "Greatest Hits", The Police "Ghost in the Machine", The Police "Zenyatta Mondatta", and countless hits of the 1970s and 1980s.

ABOUT THE AUTHOR

Nicole Kobrowski is co-owner of Unseenpress. com, Inc., which was founded in 2001. She and her husband Michael started the business because of their interest in the paranormal and their love of history. She has written professionally for over 35 years, including true paranormal, true crime, history, fiction, international relations, and English as a Second Language. Being a paranormal enthusiast for over 40 years, she has done investigation work in many areas including spirit photography, electronic voice phenomenon, and automatic writing. In addition to her work in the paranormal field, Nicole is an adult educator. Currently, she lives in her "über" haunted home with her husband and Lyla, her bad ass cat.

Nicole loves hearing from her readers. If you wish to contact Nicole she can be reached via e-mail at customerservice@unseenpress.com.

OTHER TITLES BY NICOLE KOBROWSKI

Published by Unseenpress.com, Inc.
(print and ebook)

- Haunted Backroads: Central Indiana
- Haunted Backroads: Ghosts of Westfield
- Haunted Backroads: Ghosts of Madison County, Indiana
- Fractured Intentions: A History of Central State Hospital for the Insane
- She Sleeps Well: The Extraordinary Life and Murder of Dr. Helene Elise Hermine Knabe
- Unseenpress.com's Official Encyclopedia of Haunted Indiana (1st and 2nd Editions)
- Unseenpress.com's Official Encyclopedia of Haunted Northern Indiana
- Unseenpress.com's Official Encyclopedia of Haunted Central Indiana
- Unseenpress.com's Official Encyclopedia of Haunted Southern Indiana
- My Dad the Racer
- Wild Innocent
- Silent Night
- Cursed Circle City (with Michael Kobrowski)
- Ghosts of Hamilton County

Published by IUPUI
Distance Learning: A Guide to System Planning and Implementation
(by Merrill, Young, and Kobrowski)

Published by Bildungsverlag EINS
- Metal Line (Instructor's guide and workbook)
- Hotel Line (Instructor's Guide)
- Englisch für Elektroberufe (Instructor's guide and workbook)
- Supply Line (Instructor's guide and workbook)
- Construction Line (Instructor's guide and workbook)

www.ingramcontent.com/pod-product-compliance
Lightning Source LLC
Chambersburg PA
CBHW071426260626
47170CB00008B/2606